THE SUMMER OF PRINCESS DIANA

ALSO BY MARTHA REYNOLDS

Chocolate for Breakfast
Chocolate Fondue
Bittersweet Chocolate

Bits of Broken Glass

A Winding Stream

The Way to Remember

A Jingle Valley Wedding
April in Galway
All's Well in Jingle Valley

WHAT READERS SAY ABOUT
MARTHA REYNOLDS' BOOKS

"[Reynolds] lives under the skin of her characters, giving voice flawlessly to personas..." —*K.C. Wilder*

"The author conveys emotion effortlessly and paints a vivid picture at every turn." —*Amazon Customer*

"I enjoy Martha Reynolds' writing because she draws you into the character's life right from the first page. You care about the characters and what happens to them."
—*Jane G*

"Anytime I pick up a book and can place myself within the story I just love it. The references to places bring me back to an earlier time. The emotions, and feelings are something I can live through with beautifully written words." —*Amazon Customer*

"Martha Reynolds is the sort of author one hopes to find. She is a natural storyteller, and if you enjoy one of her books, you are sure to enjoy them all."
—*Amazon Customer*

The Summer of Princess Diana

Martha Reynolds

THE SUMMER OF
PRINCESS DIANA

CHAPTER ONE
Summer, 1976

The shrill screech of tires on the road in front of Diana's house caught her attention. One minute, she'd looked away for one minute! Dropping the latest copy of *Glamour*, she bolted from her lounge chair and ran barefoot across the front lawn to the road. Chip and Cam were in their Big Wheel, Chip at the wheel and younger Cam standing up behind him, his tiny hands on Chip's narrow shoulders. Two towheads on a primary-colored trike, in the middle of the road. A mustard-yellow convertible was stopped just a foot from the boys in the road. Diana's feet skimmed the finely manicured grass and skidded to a stop at the edge of the street.

"Hey!" She grabbed Chip, six, by the arm and tugged him, his brother, and their toy tricycle onto the grass.

"You shouldn't let them play in the street." The voice belonged to the man behind the wheel of the convertible. His eyes were hidden behind mirrored aviator sunglasses, and his dark oily hair glistened under the sun. So did the gold watch on his wrist. Diana squinted at him. He looked like Tom Selleck in *Magnum*, especially with the mustache. He was wearing a pale pink shirt, unbuttoned to show a thatch of dark chest hair. He waggled his index finger from Diana to the boys before giving them a bared-teeth grin. The woman sitting next to him flipped down her sun visor and twisted a hot-pink lipstick up from a shiny gold tube, then pursed her lips and reapplied. Her copper hair and bronze shoulders were as buffed and polished as the burnished teakettle that sat on their kitchen stove.

"Sorry," Diana muttered. The man lowered his sunglasses to look at her. He grinned again, then shifted gears and sped away. "Boys, what were you doing? You know you're not supposed to play in the road. You could have been killed!" Her little brothers were like puppies sometimes.

Cam, four, giggled. "We won't get kilt! Chippy has magic powers!" He slapped his little hands on Chip's shoulders.

"Yeah, okay. Well, get your Big Wheel and your magic powers back to the house. It's almost lunchtime." She walked behind the boys as Chip pedaled the tricycle up the long curving driveway, around to the back of the house and the play area where the boys were supposed to stay. "Go on inside and wash your hands. Trudy has lunch ready. I think it's your favorite, tuna fish sandwiches."

"With pickles?" Chip asked. His brown eyes were big and round in hopeful expectation. Diana gently pushed the white-blond hair from his forehead.

"Of course. Go on now."

Diana let the screen door bang shut and stood on the back step, listening to the high-pitched, singsong voices of her brothers. She was supposed to watch the boys, keep them safe, and she'd failed. Caught up in an article in *Glamour* titled "How to Make Peace with your Mother," she had neglected her duties and let them pedal their tricycle into the road, where they could have been hit by a car, or worse. The worst didn't happen, but Diana couldn't bear to imagine life without Chip and Cam. With just her and her parents.

TWO
February 1981

Diana Driscoll was folding cotton sweaters in the Pappagallo store on Bellevue Avenue in late February when she learned from a customer that Britain's Prince Charles, heir to the throne, age thirty-two, had found his bride, someone named Lady Diana Spencer, age nineteen. Diana was mildly annoyed that someone else had that information before she did, especially since she devoured any news that had to do with the royal family. The customer was speaking with Gwendolen, the manager of the shop, who always went by Gwendolen and never by Gwen. Gwendolen reminded Diana of a well-bred bay horse. Her elongated face had a prominent jaw and chin, a mouth full of big teeth that Diana was sure were false, and her dark hair had a patch of white just above her right temple. Diana assumed that was the way she wanted it.

"How do you know? About the engagement?" Diana asked, once she had caught the eye of the customer. Tall and bored-looking, the shopper touched a beige-gloved hand to her hair, which was a perfectly sealed and lacquered helmet of ash blonde. She turned her attention away from Gwendolen to face Diana. She looked Diana up and down, as if appraising her, deciding whether she would allow her, Diana, just a clerk in the Pappagallo store, to know what she knew about the royal engagement.

"I have friends in London," the woman replied, as if the mere effort of talking about it was a bore. "It's been announced today." She turned her back to Diana and selected a skirt from a display—a new arrival, Diana almost said, before realizing the woman would probably give a withering, 'I'm aware' look. The customer spoke with Gwendolen, but in a lower voice, presumably so Diana wouldn't hear and butt in again.

Always a royal watcher, Diana was particularly interested in the engagement. There had been rumblings about a young woman, a nursery school assistant, named Diana who had seemingly caught the eye of the prince. *Who was this young woman that had snared the world's most eligible bachelor?*

Diana bought every magazine she could find that featured the couple on its cover. She stared at the official photograph—Lady Diana in a cobalt-blue skirt suit and white bow blouse, that massive sapphire engagement ring on her left hand.

Diana read that the future princess bit her nails. *Well, of course she does.* She's nineteen and engaged to the future king of England! Prince Charles stood behind Lady Di in the photograph, one hand resting lovingly on her shoulder, smiling. He looked happy. Lady Di looked nervous. The photographers had been following her for weeks, ever since there was a whiff in the air that she might be the one. But Diana hadn't been privy to any of the British magazines; if she had, maybe she'd have known about the engagement before that snooty customer.

A week after the royal engagement, in early March, Diana's mother Evelyn was admitted to Seaside Recovery Center. Again. She would be in "rest and recovery" for three weeks. Last time it was just a week. Diana asked Gwendolen if she could work extra hours at the Pappagallo store. Gwendolen raised her perfectly arched eyebrows but acquiesced. Win Driscoll, Diana's father, hired a Swedish exchange student to help around the house and keep an eye on Chip and Cam in the afternoons. Her name was Astrid, her hair was strawberry-blonde and so long she could sit on it, and she never wore socks or shoes in the house. While she was looking after the boys, apparently Win Driscoll was looking after Astrid.

Diana returned home from work one afternoon, earlier than expected, and surprised her father and Astrid in the kitchen. Astrid was sitting on the counter (*the counter! naked! Her bare bum on the kitchen counter!!*) and Diana's father was standing in between Astrid's legs. He was holding her ankles and wearing socks and his dress shirt. Thankful that his shirt covered most of his bare bottom, Diana stood frozen in her spot at the entryway to the kitchen. As Astrid slid off the counter (*slid! naked off the counter!*) and slipped a tank top over her bare breasts, she glanced quickly at Win before bounding out of the kitchen like a surprised gazelle.

"Oh! Darling! You're home early! I thought you were working late this evening," he said, tugging at his shirt and looking around for his trousers.

Diana held a hand to her eyes. "Daddy, don't. Don't turn around, please. Oh my god."

With little more than a grunt, Win Driscoll grabbed his pants from a nearby chair and made a hasty exit. Diana stood in her place, her hand still shielding her eyes from a scene she would never be able to unsee. Her father. And Astrid, whose legs were tanned and muscular and long. Astrid, who maybe should have sat on her hair instead of the kitchen counter. Diana opened a cupboard under the sink and took out the bottle of Windex.

❧

Her father's indiscretion cost him a generous severance for Astrid, who packed up and departed the Driscoll house by taxi before dinner.

Later that evening, after she'd put the boys to bed and told them that Astrid had to go home to see her mommy, Diana confronted her father in his den. "Daddy, Astrid was only eight months older than me. Did you know that?" She flattened her palms on his desk and leaned toward him. She wanted to invade his personal space, make him feel a fraction of the discomfort he had made her experience earlier in the day.

"Honey, it was just a little fun. Nothing, really. I've been lonely without your mother." Looking up at his daughter, Win tried the charm that had worked so well, first on Evelyn Lanzi, a dark-haired and curvaceous waitress at an Italian restaurant in Providence, then on all the many other women who had followed, before and after he'd married Evelyn. Diana was aware of her father's flirtatious manner. She'd even guessed that he hadn't been completely faithful to her mother, whose depression hung over the house like the low clouds over Newport harbor. But seeing it, and with Astrid (*naked on the kitchen counter!*) brought Diana to the conclusion that she had to get away. She dropped into a soft leather chair opposite his desk. The grandfather clock against the wall ticked in rhythm to her heart as she pondered her next move. Her father poured himself a generous three fingers of scotch, while Diana sipped Tab from a can.

"I don't believe it was nothing, Daddy. And I don't want to talk about it, not another word. She's gone and I'm glad." Diana set the sweating can on her father's desk, but not before Win slipped a leather and cork coaster beneath it. "Mommy is being released in the morning. I'm going to pick her up, then take her to lunch at Sardella's. Gwendolen told me I could come in to work at three." With a pointed look at her father, she added, "It's *tomorrow* they're open late, Daddy. You probably thought it was tonight."

Win cleared his throat. "Thank you, darling girl. And as far as that tiny incident..."

"It didn't happen." Diana regarded her father with narrowed eyes. He was still so handsome at forty-eight. He could pass for Harrison Ford's older brother. Win Driscoll played racquetball at the club three days a week, swam laps in the pool, and still had plenty of hair, even if there were a few silver threads mixed in with the pale gold. Charming. Rakish, some would say. He was born into moderate wealth and had increased it aggressively by investing wisely. His clients loved him for making them wealthier, too.

"Daddy," Diana ventured, confident in her belief that keeping silent about her father's 'indiscretion' could get her what she wanted. "I'd like to go to London this summer. Prince Charles and Lady Diana are getting married in July and I want to be there. It's an historic event." She paused, took a breath. Then she decided to go for broke.

"And Mulligan's in Switzerland for the rest of the school year, so I thought I'd go visit her first." She tucked her hands under her thighs and waited. Did he think she would tell her mother about him and Astrid? If she did, Diana knew it could send her mother into an even deeper depression, and she wouldn't want that. But her father was on the ropes.

Win Driscoll stroked his strong dimpled chin. He'd grown a beard and mustache the previous year and had talked about growing it back, even though Evelyn had said she hated it. He smiled at his daughter. "Switzer-land *and* London?"

Diana nodded. "I've got my degree and I've been applying for jobs, real jobs. The art museum said there weren't any positions available right now, except for volunteering. I'm saving the money I make at Pappa-gallo, even though it isn't that much. But if I'm going to London, I don't want to pass up the chance to see Mul-ligan while she's in school in Switzerland." She hated waiting on the old, blue-haired Newport doyennes who came into Pappagallo, thinking the preppy combination of bright pink and Kelly green might restore their long-gone youth. Plus, her father owed her now. She didn't want to say that, though, and back him into a corner. Win was still a fighter when he was confronted.

"What about you and Myles? What's going on there?"

Back on Christmas Eve, Diana had broken up with Myles Olyphant, weary of his neediness. She wanted a take-charge boyfriend, not a human-redemption proj-ect. Myles was on her parents' approved list of suitors, but Diana wasn't interested in an arranged match with one of Newport's scions. "We haven't really talked lately. I don't know, Daddy, I don't think he's the one."

"He comes from a good family, sweetheart. You could do a lot worse than Myles."

"Sometimes that's not enough, Daddy. You of all people should understand that." Win's choice of Evelyn Lanzi as his bride caused a crevasse of friction in his family, but he hadn't cared at the time. At least that was the story his parents had told her.

"Besides, Myles is...oh, I can't explain it." She could, but not to her father. She felt absolutely nothing when she looked at Myles. "We're just not a match, that's all." His unkissable mouth, the way he parted his hair, the wingtips! All superfluous, Diana was aware, but it completely detracted from any appeal his considerable inheritance might have.

"All right, kitten. It sounds like you've given this adventure some thought." Win poured another drink and held out the bottle to his daughter. She wrinkled her nose and lifted her can of Tab.

"I've looked into it. I could fly over next month, stay with Mulligan until the end of June, then fly to London for the rest of the summer. I'd be back in late August," she added. *Unless I meet my own prince. Or at least find a meaningful job, maybe in one of the British art museums.*

"And you've corresponded with Dorothy about this? About staying with her?"

"Daddy, don't call her Dorothy. She hates it."

"She's a young lady from a very good family. That's her name. She can't go through life being called Mulligan."

"Of course she can. It's 1981. And yes, she'll be fine with me staying with her. I'll write to her tonight."

Win stared into his glass, as if all the answers to life were swirling around in the amber liquid. He raked a hand through his hair before raising his eyes to Diana's.

"And your passport is still current? All right then, I'll see what I can do about getting you someone to stay with in London."

"Oh Daddy, thank you!" Diana rushed around the massive oak desk to hug her father. He patted her head but did not embrace her in return. Why was it so difficult for him to show affection to her or her mother? He'd had no problem with Astrid. Diana pulled back and stood over him, looking down.

"Give the travel dates and whatever else you need to Irene. She'll handle everything."

Diana turned to leave her father's den, casting a look at the fine furnishings in the room. While their home was modest compared to the mansions on Bellevue, the seven-bedroom, five-bathroom house on Hanson Avenue was still elegant and stately. There was a working fireplace in nearly every room, multiple porches with views of the Atlantic Ocean. So many rooms to play in, Diana had a separate playroom when she was little, her own bathroom and porch. It was hard for Diana to understand why her mother was so sad.

THREE

April 1981

Diana had only been on an airplane once before, when the family flew to Palm Beach in 1973 to spend the Christmas holidays with her grandmother on her father's side. Diana remembered the plane ride as the best part of the entire trip. One school excursion to Quebec by bus two years ago didn't count as international travel, but Diana had a passport and a stamp in it to prove she had been out of the country.

The flight from Boston to Zurich departed at nine o'clock at night and took seven hours. Diana was annoyed that her father's secretary Irene hadn't ordered a first-class ticket. Why hadn't she bargained for and insisted on it? As she boarded with the masses, she had to pass through the first-class section. There were a few empty seats, roomy seats occupied by well-dressed people. She briefly considered asking the flight attendant to upgrade her ticket and charge it to her father's account but realized it probably wouldn't work. Why was everyone else forced to walk through the first-class cabin? It just made the rest of the passengers resentful. Diana paused, glancing up at the letters and numbers above the seats. 31D, the end seat of a middle row of four. Two seats at each window, four seats in the middle. Crammed in like sardines. *Should I be sitting in first class? Am I that special?* As she seated herself, Diana realized she would be in the coach cabin if she'd had to pay for the ticket herself. It was only through her father's wealth that she lived the way she did. But she didn't want to be like everyone else. Wasn't she a princess? That's what her father always told her. *"You're my princess, Diana."* Now she had real competition—Lady Diana Spencer was about to become a true-life princess.

She watched the other passengers stow small bags in overhead compartments, shrug out of jackets, wedge themselves into their seats, sometimes rising again to allow another passenger in. She wondered who would occupy the seat next to her. *Not a prince, that's for sure.* She stopped herself. *Oh, get a grip, Diana. You're on your way to Switzerland. You'll see your best friend and hang out for a couple of months. Then it's off to London and the royal wedding*. Diana smiled at the thought. She was lucky. She missed Mulligan and couldn't wait to catch up. Letters that took a week to reach her, and vice versa, weren't good enough.

"Hello," a male voice said. The airplane was nearly full. Diana lifted her gaze to meet the eyes of a man. Slender, with soft features. Pale skin. His hair was like hay, and a mess. Too much hair for such a narrow face, she thought. He was almost delicate, elfin.

"Hi," she said. "I'm Diana." Might as well be friendly.

She stood in the aisle to allow him in. He had seat 31E, next to her on her right. The other two seats in the row were taken by an elderly couple.

"Josef." He offered his hand in greeting. Diana, flustered, took it in hers. His skin was warm and slightly damp. She pressed her palm into her skirt.

"You go to Zurich?" he asked. A strong, masculine voice that didn't match the man. And an accent. What was it?

Diana bit back a sarcastic reply. Maybe he thought she'd have a connecting flight. "Yes, Zurich. You?"

"Zurich first, then to Vienna," he said.

His English was good, but Diana did not wish to converse all evening. When the flight attendant offered free headphones, she greedily grabbed the plastic bag and tore into it like a hungry animal. By the time she'd figured out where to plug in and selected a channel of contemporary music, Josef was engrossed in a book. Diana glimpsed the title—*Die Blechtrommel*. She had no idea what it meant.

She slept a little but woke often, while Josef next to her slept soundly. He had curled himself into his seat like a snail into his shell, facing away from her. He blew out small breaths in a rhythmic pattern.

The window shades were all down, and she had no proximity to a window from her middle-row seat. Her wristwatch read ten minutes to two. Six hours ahead, she told herself. So...ten minutes to eight in the morning. The plane should touch down in two hours. After adjusting her watch, she closed her eyes and listened to Josef breathe.

There were noises coming from the front of the plane. The sound of plates and silverware and glasses drifted down the aisle to seat 31D. Diana's stomach grumbled, and she recalled passing up the offered meal hours earlier. She needed to pee. The cabin was still darkened, but she could make her way toward the back and the lavatory. Carefully she rose from her seat and banged her head on the compartment above. "Ow!"

Josef woke with a jerk of his body and turned in his seat. Eyeing her as if for the first time, he mumbled, "Good morning."

"Hi," she whispered. "Sorry, didn't mean to wake you."

"It's okay." Josef uncurled himself, looked at his own wristwatch, and straightened himself into a sitting position. He smiled at her. "We land soon?"

"Soon." Diana grabbed her purse from under her seat and staggered on cramped legs to the bathroom. At least she could freshen up before they landed. Mulligan had written that she couldn't meet her at the airport, but had sent explicit instructions about getting to the town of Fribourg, two hours south of Zurich.

❧

The airport was teeming with people. She stood in line at Customs, clutching her passport in her hand. When it was her turn, she stepped forward and slid her passport through a small opening to the uniformed man on the other side of the glass. He glanced up at her, unsmiling, and asked her, in heavily accented English, how long she planned to stay in Switzerland.

"Until the end of June," Diana replied. "I'm staying with a friend."

He gave her a curt nod, then stamped her passport and slid it back to her.

She took two steps to her right and peeked at the passport. SCHWEIZ, it read. ZURICH FLUGHAVEN underneath, and the date. A shiver of anticipation ran through her. She followed the signs to collect her matching suitcases, then found an information booth, where she purchased a train ticket to the town of Fribourg.

Her train was at noon, so she stopped to change the American dollars she had brought with her to Swiss francs. Diana had asked her father to get her American Express Travelers Cheques, but instead he had handed her an American Express credit card, told her to keep it safe, and to use it when she needed cash.

At two o'clock, Diana stepped off the train in Fribourg, a university town with easily navigable streets and a Gothic cathedral as its focal point. She handed a sheet of paper with Mulligan's address written on it to an employee at the ticket office and was given directions in French, spoken so rapidly she couldn't keep up.

"I don't understand," she blurted, then tried to say the same thing in French. The man at the ticket window scowled at her, heaved a loud sigh of exasperation, then stood and called to a woman working at the next window. She looked over, but shook her head. The man leaned close to Diana, fixed his beady eyes on her, and spat each word into her face. "Turn. Left. At. The. Corner." He raised a meaty arm to point to the right.

"*Merci*," Diana whispered, turning away, her face hot with shame. Why did he have to be so rude? Had he never encountered someone who didn't speak his language? She paused outside the train station, gulping in air redolent of diesel fumes, and recalled one hot July day years ago, when her mother had yelled at Nydia, the woman who cleaned their house. Nydia's English was marginal at best, and apparently she hadn't cleaned the boys' bathroom to Evelyn's exacting specifications.

Diana remembered the scene and shivered, in spite of the warm April sun. Her mother had raised her voice, then just as swiftly lowered it. She had leaned in close to Nydia, the way the man at the ticket booth had done, and enunciated each word as if Nydia were a two-year-old, until the poor woman dissolved into tears.

"I'm sorry, Nydia," Diana said softly to the air. "I'm so sorry."

FOUR

Diana pressed the buzzer at the door of the house. Within minutes, a smartly dressed woman, whose age Diana guessed to be around forty, possibly younger, opened a heavy oak door.

"Hello! You must be Diana! Welcome, I'm Pascale." Seeing Diana's puzzled expression, she laughed and opened the door wider. "Your friend Mulligan lives here, in an apartment at the rear of my house. Did she not tell you? No matter, she let me know you'd be arriving today." Pascale checked her watch. "She'll be back in an hour or so, I believe. Here, let me help you with your luggage."

"You speak English," Diana said. She wanted to hug the woman. Pascale, with her stylish bobbed hair and red lips, laughed. Her skin was as fine as porcelain, but when she smiled, there were the finest of lines at the corners of her gray eyes.

"Yes, of course. Most of us do, you know. I was educated in England, so I have the advantage, I suppose. Come, let's get you to your room." Pascale walked with purpose down a long hallway lined with framed oil paintings of landscapes and mountains. She stopped in

19

front of a white door with a small painted sign attached that read D. MULLIGAN. Diana reached out to touch her fingers to the plaque. *Hey, Mull.*

"Mulligan, I'm here," she said aloud.

Pascale laughed again, and Diana noticed dimples in her cheeks. "Yes, I also call her Mulligan, as instructed. She does not care for the name Dorothy."

"This is true."

Pascale unlocked the door and gestured for Diana to enter first. Dropping her suitcases to the floor, Diana took in her surroundings. Simple but elegant, she thought. They stood in what was the living room, which was furnished with two long sofas and two upholstered chairs, all in shades of brown and blue. A woven rug in dark red and navy blue covered most of the parquet floor. In the quiet, Diana heard the rhythmic ticking of not one, but two, clocks. She spied one of the clocks on a table, a small timepiece under a glass dome. Four golden balls twisted and twirled at the base of the clock.

There was a wooden table and four ladderback chairs at the far end of the room, next to a window. Two candlesticks and two white tapers stood in the middle of the table, which was polished to a gleaming shine. All clean and minimalist, Diana noted.

"I will leave you now, Diana. But I'm right at the front of the house, so if you need anything, please don't wait to find me." She used her hand to smooth her already smooth hair before letting herself out.

With Pascale gone, Diana was free to explore. Behind

the living room was a bedroom with a bed somewhere between a single and a double, covered in a puffy, sky-blue duvet. A tall, fine-grained wood dresser with four drawers stood against one wall, and Diana sniffed the air. A bottle of Mulligan's scent, Shalimar, sat on the dresser, its urn-shaped container distinctive and instantly recognizable. There was also a small, white ceramic bowl that held two pairs of earrings: silver hoops and gold studs. A jar of Nivea cream.

Diana stood in front of a tall armoire of the same polished wood, whose front was painted blue and yellow and orange. She opened the door and recognized some of Mulligan's clothes. White and pink Oxford shirts, a navy-blue skirt, another in khaki, one Lilly Pulitzer dress in turquoise and pink, black flats, snow boots, white sneakers. Mulligan. She spent her money carefully, once telling Diana that she'd rather own just one pair of well-made shoes than four pairs of trendy heels. Diana couldn't imagine; she bought what she wanted and never considered the price. For her high school graduation, Diana's father had presented her with a white Honda Prelude convertible. He never said a word about her spending, and she never imagined it to be a problem.

Before she could unpack her own suitcases, Diana heard Mulligan at the door, and she catapulted herself into her friend's open arms.

"I've missed you, you idiot," she cried, hugging Mulligan hard.

"You too, dope!" Mulligan replied, laughing. "How

was the trip? Luxurious, I'll bet." She pulled away and rested her hands on Diana's shoulders, appraising her at arm's length.

"*Not*. My father—or more likely, his secretary—dumped me in coach."

"How terribly awful for you." Mulligan dripped sarcasm, then dropped down to the sofa, draping one long leg over the arm.

"Oh, come on, Mull. You know what I mean."

"Not really. I've never flown first class." She gave Diana a pointed look.

Diana lowered her eyes. "Okay. Well, actually, the flight was okay. I sat next to a guy who was headed to Vienna. He slept for most of the flight. I don't think I slept at all. I should probably take a nap. I was just waiting for you to come home."

"No, you can't nap. If you do, you'll be awake at two in the morning. I'll help you get settled, then we'll take a walk around town. We're invited to dinner at Páscale's tonight. She's nice, isn't she?" Mulligan unzipped one of Diana's matching suitcases.

"Yeah, she is. And her English is good."

Mulligan looked up. "Of course it is. Most people here speak English. Come on, help me out here. I made room in the armoire and there are two drawers for you. How much stuff did you bring, anyway?"

"Ha ha, Mull. My blue jeans, my black jeans, my white jeans, sneakers..."

"Got it, got it," Mulligan said with a dismissive wave of her hand."

FIVE

Only a week after she had arrived in Fribourg, Diana was already bored. Mulligan went to the university every day, Monday through Friday, and Diana couldn't see any reason to go with her, so she was left to explore on her own. She had walked down cobblestone streets to the *basse-ville,* replete with tightly packed houses, bridges, and fountains, and once she had walked around and seen everything, she rode the funicular to the newer upper part of town, *la neuveville*. The ride in the pale green cabin of the funicular smelled awful, though, and she later learned that gravity and sewage water pulled the lower car upwards. Mulligan told her it was historical. Too bad, Diana had replied, it smelled like stale pee, and worse. From that point on, she walked, using the covered stairs next to the funicular. *Better for my legs and bum*, she told herself.

She visited the gothic St. Nicholas Cathedral, twice, but would not climb the 500-year-old tower to the top, in spite of the benefits to her posterior. There was a guided tour available, but Diana preferred to explore on her own. She spent one afternoon in the natural history museum, on a day that the local elementary school had sent over dozens of little kids. She walked back and forth over the covered wooden bridge, and read a sign in German, French, and English that the original bridge dated back to the mid-13th century. Mulligan had taken her to the Villars chocolate factory, where they watched the cacao beans be cleaned, roasted, crushed, and kneaded. They sampled white, milk, and dark varieties, and Diana agreed that it was the best chocolate she had ever tasted. They took a tour of the Cardinal beer brewery, and they each drank two glasses, although Diana didn't care much for beer and burped all the way back home.

On the first Saturday in May, Diana and Mulligan were enjoying the first real spring day in Fribourg by sitting in the sun at the Plaza Café. They weren't the only ones, as it seemed as though the entire population of Fribourg had moved outdoors, occupying all of the tables at all of the cafés and bistros up and down the rue de Romont. Families filled the green space at Grand-Places, and there were picnics, soccer balls, Frisbee. Vélos buzzed up and down the streets. Diana noticed that there was a feeling of excitement and anticipation, the same way her town of Newport came alive in the spring. Except that there was no harbor full of sailboats and yachts, no Ocean Drive, no Salas' restaurant for a steaming plate of linguine with red clam sauce.

A little boy of about two years old ran in and around the twenty or so crowded tables outside the café.

The pleasant, harmless scene was pierced by the sound

of screeching tires. Diana tensed, waiting for the horrible sound of metal crashing into metal, or worse, the thud of a car hitting a person. Mulligan was on her feet, as were some of the other patrons at the café. Diana's view was blocked by a tall hedge at her shoulder, but Mulligan had risen quickly and was standing some yards away, her hand shading her eyes from the bright sun. She returned to their table in minutes and pronounced, "Nothing."

"Nothing?" Diana was incredulous. "It sure sounded like something."

Mulligan shrugged. "That little boy we saw running around the tables? He ran into the street, but the car stopped." Her eyes rolled skyward. "His parents, or grandparents, I don't know, are the ones down there at the end, see?" She pointed to a couple at the far end of the *terrasse*.

Diana looked. A man and woman sat at a table in the full sun, and the little boy was on the woman's lap. Her hand was in the boy's chocolate-colored curls while the other hand held a cigarette. The man was smoking, too. They looked too old to be the little boy's parents.

"Well, that was the most excitement I've had since I got here," Diana said, as life returned to normal and the café buzzed again with the sounds of happy people. She sighed and raised her glass to her lips.

Mulligan sat down heavily and shook her head. "Diana, you need to get over yourself. You've been here for two weeks. What did you expect? I've got school until June, and I can't blow off my classes because you're bored." Mulligan spread her hands on the table, palms down. Her nails were short and unpainted, and the only jewelry she wore was a silver filigree ring on her right hand. She sat looking down at her hands, then looked up. Diana saw something hard in her eyes. "What is it you want?"

Diana flinched at her friend's sharp words. "Sorry. No, really, I'm sorry, Mull. I don't want you to be sick of me. I just thought we'd be able to travel around, see the Alps, eat fondue, that kind of stuff. This town is dead by nine o'clock! I think I've seen everything here, and I guess I just thought we'd be able to have fun together." She chewed her lower lip. This wasn't turning out to be at all what Diana had expected.

Mulligan let out a tired sigh as her shoulders dropped. "That's just how it is, Di. Fribourg is a sleepy little university town. I have to get through my classes, especially the ones that are taught in French. Did you know I'm taking a course in Medieval Studies, taught *in French*? It's awful! We have a seminar on Wednesday evenings, where the professor goes over the coursework in English, thank god."

"I didn't know. Jeez, Mull." Diana had never considered taking a semester abroad, and knowing about Mulligan's foreign-language classes, she was glad she hadn't. Imagine! Although Diana's classes in art history hadn't been bad, if they'd been taught in Italian, she'd have flunked, for sure.

"Plus, I just had a six-week break before you arrived. Why did you come so early? I mean, the wedding in

London isn't until the end of July. You've got nearly three months until then." Mulligan pushed her empty glass toward the center of the table and stood, a signal to Diana that it was time to go. "You know, Diana, you should travel around Europe. It's perfectly safe to travel by yourself. And you've got plenty of money." The last sentence was delivered with a bitterness Diana hadn't heard previously. Growing up, Diana always knew that Mulligan's family wasn't as wealthy as Diana's, but it never bothered her. And it never seemed to bother Mulligan. But maybe it had.

Diana stood as well, and handed a ten-franc note to the waiter, who was hovering near their table. As he dug for change in the pocketed apron he wore around his slim waist, Diana waved him off. He gave her a curious look, then bowed and scurried away. "I'd rather travel with you, though," she said to Mulligan.

"That's not an option. Sorry." Mulligan dug in her pocket, produced a cloth-covered elastic, then gathered her thick golden hair in her hands and secured a ponytail at the back of her head. "And listen, I wanted to tell you something. I know you have a lot of money, but there's no need to tip here. You just gave the waiter ten francs. The total for our drinks was less than five."

"So? I'm generous." *Did Mulligan have to complain about everything?* "I'm just trying to help, Mull."

"Yeah, but that's not how it's *done*, Diana. It's not expected. Well, maybe now it will be."

Mulligan turned to walk away, but Diana grabbed

her friend's arm. "Mull, I don't get it. What's the problem? Why are we fighting?"

Mulligan led the way out to the street. She turned to Diana, but with her sunglasses on, Diana couldn't read her expression. The tone of her voice was unmistakable, though.

"Could you just *try* to acclimate?" She lowered her voice to a near-whisper. "I make an effort not to stand out as an American. Don't overtip. Don't tip at all! You don't have to impress me, I already know you're loaded."

"Whoa, hold on a minute. I wasn't trying to impress you, Mull! I was trying to help the waiter out."

"But that's just it, Diana. He doesn't need it. There's no tipping here, because the people who work in restaurants are paid a decent wage. We could have sat at that table all day, with just one drink, and it wouldn't have mattered. Can you understand that?"

"Okay, well, I didn't know," Diana muttered.

"Well, now you do." Mulligan softened her voice. "Look, I know you're just trying to be nice. And you paid for my drink, so thanks." She linked her arm through Diana's. "If you don't want to travel through Europe by yourself, I really think you should make a day trip somewhere. It would do you good."

"Do us both good, right?" She paused, and when Mulligan turned her face to Diana, she lowered her sunglasses. "Mull, my French is terrible. People are mean when you don't speak their language." Diana felt her face grow warm, remembering Nydia.

"They're not mean, Di. They just want you to try. You know some French, so just give it a try. Don't go sashaying into a store, expecting everyone to speak English."

"I don't sashay."

"Sometimes you do."

"Wow," Diana said, shaking her head. "I didn't even realize."

"I know. But now you realize." Mulligan threw her arm around Diana's shoulders and drew her close. They walked past the bank, the hair salon, the train station. "Look. I love having you around, I really do. And I'm sorry I can't play with you during the week. But I don't want *you* to be miserable, either. You know, you could take the train to Bern. It's only twenty minutes, direct, and there's lots of shopping there."

Diana nodded. "Okay. And I'm sorry, Mull, I don't want to be a jerk. I guess I'm just finding my way. I am really happy to be here with you."

"Hey, tomorrow we can take the train to Bern together if you want. It's Sunday—no work on Sunday."

"No shopping, either? Isn't everything closed?"

"It'll be okay. Come on."

SIX

On Monday, shortly after Mulligan had left for the university, Diana washed the coffee cups and made up the sofa bed, returning it to its regular position. She cleaned the sink and the table. Without a person to come in and clean, she and Mulligan kept the apartment neat. Well, Mulligan was neater, but Diana tried to do her part.

Resolved to take Mulligan's advice about traveling throughout Switzerland, she picked up the green time-table book from the side table and flipped through the pages, searching for a day trip. Somewhere, anywhere. Mulligan had suggested Lausanne, a forty-minute train ride to the south.

That's manageable, she thought. There were no clouds in the sky to suggest rain, but Mulligan had said the weather was always changeable. A good day to head to Lausanne, with her umbrella, just in case. Perhaps have lunch by the lake.

A rapid knock on the door startled her. "Diana? Are you there?" Diana opened the door to find Pascale, her face tight and worried, two vertical lines between her eyebrows.

"*Bonjour*, Pascale. Everything okay?"

"Diana, a telegram just arrived. For you." Her hand trembled as she held it out.

A telegram? *Who died*, Diana wondered, and for a split second, really just a fraction of a split second, she hoped that if it was one of her parents, it was her mother and not her father. *I'm awful for even thinking that. I don't want anything to happen to my parents. Maybe her miserly old grandmother in Florida.*

"Should I leave you alone?" Pascale asked quietly.

Diana looked at her with wide eyes. *Someone has definitely died*, she thought. But she didn't want Pascale to leave. She couldn't be by herself with that kind of news.

"No, please stay, Pascale. Telegrams are always bad news, aren't they?"

Without waiting for a reply, Diana opened the telegram, willing herself to breathe normally.

DIANA. PLS CALL HOME IMMEDIATELY. YOUR FATHER HAS BEEN ARRESTED. MOTHER.

Diana read the lines twice, then held the piece of paper away from her face, as if it had a poisonous quality. She couldn't pull air into her lungs and heard herself gasping as she bent at the waist. Pascale took the telegram from Diana's hand and read it, then knelt on the rug next to where Diana was also on her knees, bent into an origami position.

"I'm so sorry, Diana," Pascale murmured. "I'm sure it must be a misunderstanding. Let me get you some water."

"It has to be a misunderstanding," Diana whispered. "Daddy's a good person. He's well-known, everybody likes him. Why would he be arrested? Arrested?!" She took the telegram from Pascale and read it again. "Why didn't she write anything else? What are the details? Look, Pascale—'your father has been arrested. Mother.' What is that?"

"Come with me, dear. You can call your mother from my telephone." Pascale stood and extended her hand to Diana. "Come on."

"What time is it at home?" Diana asked as she rose to her feet.

Pascale touched a fingertip to the watch on her wrist. "We're six hours ahead, so it's only three in the morning there. Would it be better to wait a few hours?"

"No, I can't wait. I need to know." Diana whooshed the breath from her lungs. "I can't believe this. Arrested for *what*?"

"Let's go call your mother."

༜

The phone rang only once, then was picked up. "Hello."

"Chip? Oh, Chip. What are you doing up? Did I wake you?"

"No, Cam's asleep but Mommy made me hot chocolate. Are you still in Switzer Land?"

"Yeah, I'm still here. Chippy, I need to speak with Mommy. Can you hand the telephone to her?"

"She went back to bed. She said you're coming home." His voice sounded so small, so innocent, through the telephone line. Diana just wanted to pull her brother through the wires and hold him in her arms.

"I really need to talk with Mommy, Chip. Please go wake her up and tell her I'm on the phone. Hurry, please." Diana glanced at Pascale, who was tending to a perfectly healthy potted fern. *I should have called collect*, Diana thought.

After what felt like an eternity, Diana heard her mother's ragged voice on the other end of the telephone line.

"Diana, we need you here at home." She sounded like someone else. Like forty years had passed.

"Mom, what happened? Where's Daddy?"

"He was arrested at work. They're holding him at the jail in town, like he's a common criminal. Come home, Diana."

Diana stood still and waited for a lengthier explanation. When none came, she lost her patience.

"Mother! Tell me what happened. Please. This is an expensive phone call." She glanced again at Pascale, who ducked her head and slipped out of the room.

"They're saying he stole money from the company."

"It's *his* company!"

"Well, from his clients. He's in jail, honey. A million dollars bail. And they took his passport. Can you get a flight today, Diana?"

"Mom, I..." Diana paced in a tight circle on the floor in Pascale's living room, twisting the telephone cord as she circled round and round.

"We're ruined. He's ruined us." Evelyn's voice was dull and flat, lifeless. The horribleness of the situation sank into Diana, covering every inch of her skin. She scratched at her neck.

"What do the boys know?" Diana asked. Chip was only eleven, Cam not quite nine.

"They know enough. I'm taking them to stay with Uncle Jimmy in Providence until this...well, I was going to say until this blows over. But I don't think it's going to blow over. It's bad, Diana. The feds don't arrest you unless they have a reason."

Diana had no words. Surely her father wasn't guilty. Surely it was just an accounting error. She didn't need to fly home for an accounting error, did she?

"Mom," she said in as soft a voice as she could, turning away to face a wall. "I hate to ask, but is there any money?"

"No. They seized everything, even the house. I can stay here, for now, but I'm going to join the boys at your uncle's house. There are TV trucks parked outside. Channel 10, Channel 12, Channel 6. I can't even let the boys play outside. We need to get away from this. I can't..."

Diana twisted the bottom button on her shirt. She twisted it so hard, it popped off in her hand. Her thoughts bumped against each other in her head. So the credit card her father had given her was no good now? She was afraid to try to use it, fearful that the Swiss police would toss her in jail, too. She didn't even have enough money to buy a plane ticket, and besides, if she was being honest, home was the last place she wanted to be. She'd rather stay in Switzerland with Mulligan.

"Mom, I have to hang up. I'll write as soon as I can. Please send me whatever news you have."

"But are you coming home, Diana?" The voice, plaintive.

"Not if I can't use the credit card," she hissed. "You need to send me money. Please." She cast a glance over her shoulder, but Pascale was still out of the room.

"I don't have money to send you, Diana. Didn't you hear what I said?"

"Well then, Mom, I can't come home. I'll write when I can. Bye." She hung up the phone, hard.

Home. The word sounded foreign.

SEVEN

Diana thanked Pascale for the use of her telephone. Should she offer to pay for the call? She should have reversed the charges. Well, she'd have to deal with that later. Pascale would understand. Diana assumed that Pascale had heard enough of her side of the conversation to deduce for herself that Diana no longer had the means to pay for anything. At least until her father's name was cleared. Because there was no way any of this was true.

She needed to find Mulligan. An urgency prickled under her skin. There was no money, and no access to money. It hurt her head to dwell on that fact. Diana had never before had to think about money, or where it came from, or how much of it there was. There was always plenty of it. She'd never had to make her own way. Her father not only had paved the way, but he had also laid down a red carpet and strewn rose petals ahead of every path she'd ever walked. A world without her father, without money, was something she wasn't prepared to face.

Pascale said nothing about the conversation, and when Diana said she'd like to take a walk to the university,

Pascale drew a little map on a piece of paper and gave her a sad smile. Diana returned to Mulligan's apartment to brush her teeth and pull a comb through her hair. *I need to talk to Mull*, she told herself. *She'll know what to do.*

Outside, dark clouds skittered across the sky. *That seems fitting.* She had neglected to take the umbrella she'd set by the door, for her day trip to Lausanne, and as she walked the route written out for her by Pascale, Diana looked to her left and noted the slanted gray lines of a storm in the distance. She assumed the skies would open and she would be drenched in minutes. Of course. What was that song her father used to sing to her when she was little? "Pennies from Heaven." Diana looked upwards to the low dark clouds and prayed for five-franc coins to pour down.

❧

After confirming with two young men on the street that she was headed in the right direction, Diana found the university. But she had no idea how to locate Mulligan. She entered the university's cafeteria and sat alone at a long table. When she overheard some students behind her speaking English, she rose and ventured over to their table.

"Hi. Excuse me. I heard you speaking English. Do you know someone named Mulligan? A woman?"

"Of course! I know her." The first student had dark, wide-set eyes and a small but noticeable scar above her left eyebrow. When she smiled, her cheeks dimpled. "I'm Renee. Sit with us."

"Thanks, I'm Diana. I'm staying with Mulligan."

"Oh! Yes, Diana. Mulligan told us you'd be visiting. We keep saying we need to have a party while you're here." Renee giggled at the thought.

"I'm trying to find her. Do you know where she is?" Diana tapped her fingers on the tabletop.

Renee looked at her wristwatch. "She should be here in a few minutes. We always eat lunch together on Monday."

At the mention of lunch, Diana's stomach growled to announce its emptiness. Did she even have enough money for lunch? She tucked her fingers into her pocket and pulled out a ten-franc note under the table. That was it. Ten francs. Her fortune.

Renee's friend had been silent, focused on an air mail letter in her hands. When she glanced up and met Diana's eyes, Diana said hello.

"I'm Pam," the other girl said. She had close-cropped hair the color of milk chocolate, and was wearing a cardigan sweater in shades of gray and red. She barely looked at Diana, focused instead on her letter.

"She misses her boyfriend," Renee explained. "She can't wait to go home and see him."

Pam touched one of her earrings, a tiny stud that Diana guessed was a diamond, miniscule as it was. "I wanted him to come and visit me, but he said he can't swing it." She finally turned her gaze to Diana. "He's saving for my ring."

"That's sweet," Diana murmured. She wondered how much Mulligan had said about her to these girls.

As if reading her thoughts, Renee said, "Mulligan told us you're staying with her until she goes back home in June, then you're flying to London for the royal wedding? That's awesome! I would give anything to be in London this summer!"

Diana swallowed hard and blinked away tears that threatened behind her eyes. Would she still be able to go to London? Her father needed to clear up the matter, the *mistake*, and fast.

"Are you okay?" Pam asked, tucking the letter in her notebook and peering at Diana's face.

"Hey, guys!" Mulligan approached the table from behind Diana. "Hey! Di, what are you doing here? I thought you were going to Lausanne today." As she came around the table, she saw Diana's face and stopped. "Hey."

"Can I talk to you? Over there?" Diana willed herself not to cry in front of the girls she'd just met.

Renee pushed her chair back from the table. "You don't have to leave. Pam and I will get our lunches while you two talk. Come on," she said. She grabbed Pam's arm and pulled her away from the table.

With the girls gone, Diana closed her eyes before speaking. Mulligan grabbed her arm.

"What is it? Did someone die?"

"My father was arrested. He's in jail!" Saying the words aloud made it worse, and Diana couldn't hold back the emotion that had been building within her since the morning. She was like a tightly wound coil let loose. "Oh my god. I just said it out loud. He's in jail, Mull."

"Wait. Why in the world is he in jail?"

"My mother said he was arrested for stealing money from his clients."

"You talked to your mother?"

Diana nodded and swiped at her eyes. "Pascale brought me a telegram this morning, right after you left. All it said was that my father was arrested. Pascale let me call home from her phone."

"Oh, Di. I'm so sorry."

"I don't know what to do, Mull." Diana held the crumpled ten-franc note in her hand. "This is all I have. I was going to hit the bank this morning before taking the train to Lausanne. My mother said they froze everything. I'm afraid to even try and use the card. And my mother wants me to fly home." She sniffed. "Mull, I don't want to go home! I had my whole summer planned." Diana beat a fist on the table. "I don't know what to do!"

Mulligan let go of Diana's arm and covered her fist with her hand. "Okay. First, we eat. One step at a time. Put your money in your pocket. I'm buying lunch. We'll figure this out. Come on." She held Diana's elbow as they walked to the food line, and passed Renee and Pam returning to their table, carrying trays.

"What's for lunch?" Mulligan asked brightly.

"*Vol-au-vent*, your favorite," Renee said.

"Ooh, good. Come on, Di, you'll love this." She escorted Diana through the cafeteria line, nodding to the woman behind the counter, indicating a plate of food for each of them. At the cashier, Mulligan paid for both of them.

"Thank you," Diana whispered. "Mull, thanks."

"Ssh. It's nothing."

Back at the table, Diana dug into her puff pastry with creamy chicken and vegetables. She didn't realize how hungry she was, and ate every speck of food on the plate. As she wiped her mouth, she felt guilty for even having an appetite.

"Diana, you are so lucky. Switzerland for three months and then London." Renee smiled, showing her dimples. "If I didn't have to go back home and work, I'd ask you if I could join you!" Seeing Diana's face, Renee added, "Don't worry, I won't! I have a job waiting for me at my uncle's factory when I get back. Still, you're lucky to be there for the wedding."

"Yeah, lucky," Pam muttered in echo. "Nice to be loaded."

Diana pushed her plate away and looked to Mulligan. Mulligan started to speak, but Diana stopped her. "It's okay." Tapping the table directly in front of Pam, Diana waited for the girl to lift her eyes to her. Then she spoke. "I'm not loaded at all. All the wealth belongs to my parents, not me. I've just been very fortunate. It's the random circumstance of birth." She opened her mouth to say more, but catching Mulligan's look, Diana stopped.

"Well, I'd love to go to London to watch the prince marry the princess. That's like once in a lifetime. A real-life fairy tale." Pam's attempt to be nice was tinged with envy, but Diana let it go.

It did flash through Diana's mind that she could ask Pam to be her traveling partner, but she quashed the idea just as quickly. Both Renee and Mulligan were heading home to jobs as soon as the school semester ended, and Pam had a boyfriend. As soon as she could make contact with her father, Diana would ask for the name and address of his business associate in London, the one he'd promised, the one he'd said would let her stay and maybe even get her a ticket to the wedding events.

Am I being delusional? Will any of this even happen now, given what's transpired? She pondered the questions silently. Diana didn't believe her father would ever steal from his clients. There was always plenty of money. Lots of money. The Driscoll family lived well. Her father wasn't as rich as some of the people who lived on Bellevue Avenue or Ocean Drive, but you'd never know it. He drove a new Mercedes every couple of years, belonged to the yacht club, the country club, and the members-only beach. Did he live above his means? Did we all? Diana lost herself in nagging thoughts.

"Well, I'm done for the day," Mulligan announced. "Diana, there's something I need to pick up. Want to come with me?"

"Sure." Diana left her lunch tray on the table until she noticed everyone else pick up their trays. She followed their lead and slid hers into a tall contraption across the room.

"Nice meeting you, Diana. Hope to see you again. I'll see what I can do about that party!" Renee waved goodbye as she and Pam left the cafeteria.

"What do you need to do?" Diana asked as she and Mulligan stepped outside. It had rained while they were eating lunch, but there was just a fine mist in the air as they made their way down the pathway to the road. The heavier clouds had lifted and the sky was still gray, but lighter.

"I think you should try the bank. Just try to make a withdrawal. It can't hurt, and you can always plead ignorance if they turn you down. If this thing just happened, maybe they won't know about it yet."

"You're right. It's not like they're going to arrest me, right? *Right*?"

"Come on."

They walked to the end of the hill, then turned left until they were standing in front of the bank. Together the girls entered the lobby. Mulligan gave Diana a little nudge. "I'll sit here and wait. Just pretend you don't know anything. It's just a typical Monday and you need cash."

Diana walked up to the available teller. "*Bonjour*," she said quietly. "I need a cash advance, please. Five hundred dollars." She slid the credit card under the glass partition, along with her passport. The teller, a woman Diana hadn't seen previously, took both documents and peered at the passport, then raised her eyes to peer at Diana. Diana remained expressionless, just like her passport picture. She'd tried to smile for that one, but the photographer had admonished her, telling her no smiling. She held the teller's gaze, as motionless as a mannequin.

"*Un moment,*" the teller said. She punched some keys on a machine in front of her and kept her eyes fixed on the screen. Then she glanced up at Diana once again and held up her index finger. She crossed over to a man sitting at a desk in an office. Diana couldn't hear a word they were saying, but the man twisted his neck to look at Diana. She could feel beads of sweat form on her upper lip, and she used her own index finger to swipe them away, hoping the bankers wouldn't notice. More sweat accumulated in her armpits and on her scalp. *Hurry up,* she pleaded silently.

The man rose from his chair in the office and opened a glass door that walled off the tellers from the customers. He smiled at her and called her name. "Diana Driscoll?"

"Yes?" She didn't know whether to approach or just stand where she was.

"Please." He gestured for her to enter the area, then led her into his office. Diana turned to look over her shoulder at Mulligan, who gave a weak thumbs-up sign.

When Diana was seated on the opposite side of his desk, the man sat. He leaned forward and rested his forearms on his desk. The man was about forty, Diana guessed, with short hair that was both black and silver, silver mostly at the temples. His chin was square and his eyes were bright blue under thick black eyebrows. His nails were trimmed and buffed, and he wore a gold band on his ring finger. He looked serious but kind. At least that was what Diana wanted to believe.

"Good day, Miss Driscoll," he said in near accentless English. "I'm Monsieur Gaffner. How are you today?"

Diana vowed to remain calm. She clasped her hands tightly in her lap. "I'm fine, thank you. Although I must admit, I've never had a problem getting a cash advance from my credit card." She looked at him expectantly.

Monsieur Gaffner steepled his fingers in front of him. "Ah, yes. You see, this card has had a freeze applied to it." At the word 'freeze,' Monsieur Gaffner unsteepled his hands and pointed all ten of his fingers in her direction.

Diana gave him a puzzled look. "A freeze? What does that mean? I don't understand."

Monsieur Gaffner looked down for a moment and shifted in his chair. "Yes, well. Perhaps it would be best for you to speak with your family about this? Are you here with them? Or alone?"

"I'm here visiting with my friend," Diana stammered. "She's just out there waiting for me."

Monsieur Gaffner cleared his throat and directed his gaze behind Diana, then pushed back in his leather chair. "I'm sorry, Miss Driscoll. I am not authorized to release any money from this card. I would urge you to telephone your..." He shook his head. "You should contact someone in your family to make other arrangements. Perhaps someone could wire the money to you."

Diana was tired of the play-acting. He believed she didn't know anything, of that she felt certain. But nothing was going to change the situation. She would not be able to get any money from the American Express card her father had so enthusiastically bestowed upon her. She met Monsieur Gaffner's kind look. "Thank you," she said quietly. "I will certainly do that."

Monsieur Gaffner stood and extended a hand. "I wish you good luck, Miss Driscoll."

Diana took his hand for the briefest of seconds before releasing it and turning to leave. She pushed the glass door open and walked through the lobby, blinking furiously. "Let's get the hell out of here, Mull."

Once they were outside and on the sidewalk, Diana slumped against the wall of a neighboring building and gulped air. "Oh god oh god oh god," she said over and over again, like a chant. Mulligan laid her hand on Diana's shoulder.

"Okay, Diana. Breathe. We need to go back home and figure things out." Mulligan looped her arm through Diana's elbow and hurried back to the apartment.

EIGHT

"I want to stay."

"You're sure?"

Diana nodded. "I really don't want to go home. Not now."

"Because I could lend you the money for a ticket. I mean, I would ask my dad."

"Nope. I'd rather stay. I'm sure that as soon as I can talk with my dad, he'll tell me that this whole nightmare is over, that it was all a mistake, that..." Diana ran her hand along the chair's upholstered arm, feeling the nubby fabric rough against her skin. "I don't know, if everything goes back to the way it was. He gets his business back, the feds apologize for being so wrong...But I *don't* want to go home. I don't think I could live in that house without my father." *With just my mother*.

"Right. Well, then. You need to get a job. Because you have no money," Mulligan said decisively.

"I'm sure everything will work out, Mull. Once they let my dad out of jail, things will go back to normal. He can wire me the money."

Mulligan inched closer to Diana from her place on

the sofa. She leaned forward, grasping her knee in her hands. "Listen to me. If you want to stay here, now, you need money. Let's focus on what is happening right now, at this minute. I can help you from time to time, but you're going to need to get a job. I can't see any other way, Di. Can you?"

"My French is awful. No one would hire me." Diana's shoulders slumped.

"You don't know that. There's got to be something you can do. Maybe an English tutor, something like that."

"I could do that." Diana sat up straighter. A tutor? Sure, she could tutor. She had helped her little brothers with their schoolwork from time to time. She'd helped out her classmates in school, too, when they couldn't figure out algebra or history. Any job that could cover her costs for the next couple of months, until she could get to London.

Mulligan lifted herself from the sofa and plugged in the electric kettle for tea. She peeled an orange, sectioned it, and placed the sections on a blue plate. When the water boiled, she filled two white ceramic mugs and brought them to the low table that sat in front of the sofa.

"You could do this, too." She gestured with her hands. "Serve coffee, tea. Don't sell yourself short, Diana. Just because you haven't *had* to work doesn't mean you're incapable of doing things."

"I have worked, Mull. I worked part-time in the Pappagallo store."

"Yeah, okay. Well, having a job here might help you."

"Help me? Help me get money?"

Mulligan held the mug to her lips, blew gently across the top, paused, then set the mug down without taking a sip. She ran her palm from her forehead, over her scalp, even though the thick curtain of blonde hair was pulled back from her face.

"Listen. I don't know anything about this situation with your father other than what you've told me." Mulligan held up her hand to stop Diana from talking. "And *you* don't know any more than what your mother told *you*. And she may not know everything." Mulligan fixed Diana with a determined stare. "Until you know the whole story, don't make assumptions, either way. Deal with what is in front of you right now. And right now, you need to find a job, because you want to stay in Switzerland, and you want to go to London. You need money. That's it, Diana. Focus."

"You're right." The weight of a painful truth sat on Diana's shoulders.

Mulligan popped an orange segment in her mouth and drummed the fingers of her left hand on her thigh. "I know where we can start."

"Where?"

"We'll check the bulletin boards at the markets. Notices for English teachers would be there."

Diana blinked at Mulligan, her mug of hot tea now cool, untouched. "I'm scared."

"I know you are, Di. Life is scary sometimes, especially when the future is uncertain. It's like riding a roller coaster, right? That anticipation as you climb to the top, knowing you're about to plunge down to the bottom. It's okay to be scared. But let's go look. One step at a time."

❧

The bulletin board at the Placette market, below ground in the five-story department store building, yielded nothing.

"All right, let's try Migros." Diana and Mulligan walked across Grand-Places to the Migros market on the corner. There they found six cards tacked to a board at the entrance to the grocery store.

"Nothing for an English tutor," Diana moaned.

"Wait. This." Mulligan put her index finger on one of the three-by-five-inch white cards. At the top it said:

Cherche à embaucher une jeune fille pour s'occuper d'un garçon de deux ans à Düdingen. Répondre à...

"You could do this, Di. It's babysitting for a two-year-old boy."

"Really?" Diana stared at the card. "A two-year-old? What is Düdingen?"

"Next town over. A village, we could walk to it. You've taken care of your brothers since they were little."

"You're right. And here it's only one. Although a little girl would have been nice."

"You could probably make enough money to get to London, if you save it. And you're staying with me until the end of June." Mulligan paused. "Maybe Pascale would even let you stay a few extra weeks until you fly to London. She rents the apartment out to a student, but the next group doesn't come until sometime in September."

"You think I have a shot at this? Even with my crummy French?"

"Sure," Mulligan said, looking off into the distant hills, still topped with snow at their peaks. "We'll ask Pascale for help with writing the letter. Be positive, Di!"

"Pascale can help me write a good letter, Mull, but eventually I'd have to have a conversation with these people."

"Don't worry about it until it happens. Let's give it a try."

"All right. I'll try." *Because*, she finished the thought silently, *if I don't, I'm heading home.*

NINE

Diana mailed a letter to the address listed on the notice. *Attention M. Brusadin*. She also sent a letter to her mother, addressed to their home in Newport, because she didn't have an address for Uncle Jimmy in Providence, and she assumed her mother would have to stop by the house in Newport to pick up the mail, that is, if the feds allowed it. In her letter, Diana let her mother know that she would be staying in Switzerland until she could get to London, "as we had planned." She inquired about her father, and mentioned that she still hoped he'd be able to provide her with a contact in London. A letter was easier than a telephone call. Besides, she couldn't ask Pascale again to use the phone to make an international call, and she was afraid her mother might not accept a collect call. If she was even still in the house. If she had already moved to Uncle Jimmy's in Providence, Diana wouldn't be able to contact her. She barely remembered her Uncle Jimmy, who had only visited them in Newport once, when Diana was in junior high school and back when Uncle Jimmy was still married. She remembered that he drank too much of her father's good scotch and said things that embarrassed her mother. Stuff about marrying up and forgetting where she'd come from. Stuff about their mother taking in laundry from the neighbors, about their father having run off with a dancer from Central Falls. Diana remembered Uncle Jimmy's wife Tonya taking the car keys away from Jimmy and driving them home in their beat-up Chevy. A little while after that, she learned that Tonya had left Jimmy to go back to her first husband, the one she had left to move in with Jimmy.

From the post office, Diana walked to the university with Mulligan, glad to have a plan for her day. Even if it was just to go to the library and read the English-language newspapers and then meet Mulligan's friends for lunch.

She entered the library and reveled in the quiet. Along one wall stood racks of newspapers—*Blick*, the German-language newspaper of Switzerland, and *Le Matin*, the daily in French, *Le Figaro* from France, and *Corriere della Sera* from Italy. She spotted *The Guardian*, England's daily, and picked it up. She found an empty table near a window and sat down to read. There was a photo of Prince Charles and Lady Di, on vacation in Scotland. In her flat-soled boots, the future princess was as tall as Prince Charles. He was dressed in a dark green sweater, and gray pleated trousers that ended at the knee, then green-gray socks and black shoes. *Nerdy*, Diana thought with a smile. Lady Di wore an adorable pink sweater with colored rows knitted in, and brown pleated trousers that either ended at the knee or were tucked into her knee-high boots. Wellingtons, Diana remembered they were called. It was a cute photo, Diana thought, with Lady Di looking like a college student. *We're pretty close in age*, Diana thought, *and I love that I resemble her so much*. Diana fingered her Lady Di haircut. *I could probably even pass for her, if I dressed the part.* She had even practiced the 'shy Di' look that had come to represent Lady Di, the looking up from under her eyelashes expression that was so endearing.

Another photograph showed the couple more formally dressed—Charles in full Scottish garb—kilt, leather pouch, and knee socks. Lady Di looked happy and lovely in heathery colors. Diana couldn't wait to go to London for the wedding. How fabulous it was going to be! What kind of a wedding dress would the future princess choose? *What will I wear?* Worries crept on top of worries—about London, the wedding, where she would stay, what she would wear, but Diana willed them away. *It'll all work out*, she promised herself.

When it was time to meet Mulligan and her friends for lunch, Diana folded the newspapers and returned them to the circulation desk. In the cafeteria, she joined Mulligan, Renee, and Pam at a table. Then Pam casually dropped a bombshell.

"So, if anyone wants to work at an exclusive private boarding school this summer, my French teacher said there's an opening." She glanced at each of them but rested her eyes on Diana. The corners of her mouth turned up in the slightest.

Renee, Diana, and Mulligan all paused, their forks in midair above plates of spaghetti Bolognese.

"Are you serious?" Mulligan asked. Pam had shoved a heavy forkful into her mouth and raised her hand as she worked her jaw. Swallowing, she looked around the table. "Anyone interested? I'd be all over it, but I can't wait to get home to my honey bunny."

"What do you know about the job?" Diana asked, measuring her words, keeping the tone of her voice neutral. Like she was just humoring Pam.

"Well," Pam began, "it's at the Eccell Institute in Montreux. The job runs from the middle of June to the third week of August, but you have to be there for all of June, July, and August." She twirled her fork around a few strands of spaghetti. "That wedding you're going to is at the end of July, right?" Without waiting for a response, she set her fork down on her plate and continued.

"The students are ages six to eighteen, but this job is for someone who can speak English—duh!—and you have to be able to teach something, like archery, or piano, or dance. Something like that." Pam took a long drink from a bottle of Sinalco, a fruity soda that Diana hadn't yet tried. She seemed awfully satisfied with herself for imparting this information, Diana thought. And why tell them anyway, if Renee and Mulligan were heading home at the end of June, and Diana was going to London in July?

"How much does it pay?" Renee asked.

"Room and board and I think Madame Theiler said it paid two thousand francs for the three months."

"Two thousand francs! Wow." Mulligan bumped her knee against Diana's under the table.

"That sounds interesting," Diana murmured. "For someone who was going to be around this summer."

"I know, right? Apparently there are all these Arabian princes who send their kids there. It's definitely a school for rich kids." Pam narrowed her eyes at Diana.

Diana looked down and picked at her spaghetti. Mulligan had offered to buy lunch again and Diana had tried to refuse, keenly aware that Mulligan wasn't rolling in extra money. But Mulligan had insisted, telling Diana it was often cheaper to eat in the university's cafeteria than anywhere else. Diana knew Mulligan watched how much she spent. It was bad enough Diana couldn't buy groceries for the apartment. By not having to buy her own lunch, Diana's lone ten-franc note remained folded in her pocket. She told herself to buy fruit, or coffee, for the apartment, even if it left her with just a few coins.

"Maybe I'll apply," Diana said softly, more to herself and Mulligan, but nothing escaped Pam.

"What about the wedding? The job goes until the end of August. You wouldn't be able to just up and leave."

"Yeah, but it's good money," Diana countered. Pam raised her eyebrows.

"It sure is," Renee chimed in. "And who knows, maybe you'd meet your own prince there!"

Diana laughed along with them and dug her nails into the palms of her hands.

⁂

Diana made a mental note to seek out Madame Theiler the following day. If Pam was right, it was an opportunity she'd be foolish to pass up. Two thousand francs for a summer in Montreux! With room and board included! She could save practically all of it. Even if she worked the months of June and July, at least she'd have enough to get to London in time for the wedding at the end of July. What did Pam know, anyway? If she made up an excuse that she had to leave, no one would be able to stop her.

But the job was for the entire summer. Words her father had drilled into her head returned— *"Diana, if you start something, it's imperative that you see it through."* Ballet lessons she had begged to quit after her instructor called out her posture in front of the class. That time she'd agreed to babysit for the Dorrance kids before getting an invitation to a party at Halsey Weatherbee's house. If she applied for and got the job in Montreux, she'd have to forget about going to London for the royal wedding. And if the situation with her father didn't change, Diana knew she'd need to figure out her next step.

Leaving Mulligan at the university for her afternoon class, Diana walked back to the apartment under a cloudless sky. Along the Rue de Weck, she passed gracious homes with manicured lawns. A flagstone path along the side of one house led to a stone wall, with stone steps leading to the rear of the home, where Diana imagined a well-dressed Swiss housewife was preparing the family's meal. Maybe roasted veal, or lamb. With crispy *rösti* potatoes and long green beans sprinkled with bits of bacon. She licked her lips as she continued down the Avenue de Tivoli, until she turned to walk past the train station. Next to Pascale's house was a lovely little *patisserie*, with a pink-and-white striped awning over the entrance and rows of exquisite baked goods in the window—*mille-feuille, baba au rhum, tartelette citron*. A customer exited the shop just as Diana walked by, and the aroma that drifted out was intoxicating—butter and sugar and cinnamon.

She wanted so much to walk inside and buy a box of pastries. Not for herself, but for Mulligan. For Pascale. Two boxes, one for Pascale and her husband, one to present to Mulligan. But the ten-franc note she had left to her name stayed in her pocket. She couldn't blow the remaining money she had on pastries, as much as her heart was in the right place. She'd need to borrow money from Mulligan. Again. Or from Mulligan's father, if he would agree to it.

Surely Edward Mulligan had read about Diana's father by now. *Of course he would know*, Diana told herself. Winfield Driscoll's arrest must have made the front page of not only *The Newport Daily News* and the *Providence*

Journal-Bulletin, but the *Boston Globe* and probably *The New York Times*, too. And Mulligan's father was a lawyer who had once worked in Newport, before he took a job in Boston and moved the family north to Massachusetts.

Oh, she wished she could talk to her father!

TEN

With Mulligan's help, Diana found Madame Theiler at the university on Thursday afternoon. The teacher was tall and reedy, with thick brown hair that she twisted into a French knot at the back of her head. Diana guessed her to be about forty, though she had clearly spent a lot of time in the sun, as her skin was taut and leathery, making her look older. Still, she smiled broadly when Diana entered her office.

"*Bonjour, madame*," Diana ventured, hoping they would not have to have the entire conversation in French.

"Diana, *bonjour*. Please, have a seat."

Relieved to hear her speak English, Diana grinned and perched on a hard chair opposite Madame Theiler. "Thank you for making time to see me."

Madame Theiler shook a cigarette from a pack on her desk and lit it, blowing smoke upwards into the air. She held the pack out to Diana, who declined with a shake of her head.

"Your friend tells me you are interested in the summer job I had mentioned to my class. Is this true?"

"Perhaps," Diana murmured. "It did sound very interesting."

"You're not a student here at university," Madame said, squinting at Diana, who shifted on the uncomfortable chair. "Still, the job is open. I have an application form here. You are required to submit the name of someone who can vouch for you." Holding the application form between the fingers of her left hand, she brought the cigarette to her thin lips and took a long drag. Her eyes never left Diana.

"Um. Well, I'm staying with Mull—Dorothy Mulligan. Her landlady might be able to vouch for me?"

"All right. We can also have a little interview here today, and if I believe you would be a good candidate for the job, you may use my name as a reference. How does that suit you?"

"Oh, yes, thank you. *Merci beaucoup.*" Diana looked at Madame with hopeful eyes.

Madame Theiler laughed, a smoky laugh that ended in a slight cough. "Very well then, Diana. Why don't you tell me about the work you have done in America, and why you think you would be a perfect employee at the Eccell Institute in Montreux?"

An hour later, Diana said goodbye to Madame Theiler and exited her office, feeling like a strand of overcooked spaghetti. When Madame had asked her what unique talent she could bring to the job, Diana had faltered. And she was sure Madame had picked up on it. After a few uncomfortable seconds of silence, Diana had suggested putting on a play. She suggested either a popular musical, if there were sufficient accommodations, or even recreating one of Shakespeare's classics. Madame had made notes in a book and nodded without telling Diana what she thought of the idea.

On Saturday, Diana received a letter from her mother, delivered to Mulligan in care of Pascale, at the address Diana had provided before leaving home. Dated a day before the telegram Diana received the previous Monday, her mother provided few details about her father's arrest, simply writing, *The current situation is intolerable for the boys and me, Diana. We will be moving in with your Uncle Jimmy until we know more. Your father is being detained and the authorities have taken possession of everything. You should plan your return trip home as soon as possible.*

There was nothing in the letter about her father's well-being, and Diana hoped he was being cared for by the authorities. After all, he was not a common criminal! Why couldn't they let him stay in his house? And why couldn't her mother stay with him, to offer support? Did she believe him to be guilty? The idea of it gave Diana pause. If your spouse can't stand by you in bad times, what are the good times worth?

She and Mulligan cleaned the apartment, then offered to clean Pascale's house. Diana had suggested it, offering to do the work herself, as a small thanks for using Pascale's phone. But Mulligan said Pascale had someone come in to clean.

"Di, let me get some studying done this morning, and then we can go somewhere this afternoon. I need a couple of hours."

"I was hoping to hear something by today, either from Monsieur Brusadin or from the school. Although the school is really a longshot. I don't think I have much of a chance getting that job."

"Be patient, Di. Something will come through."

Diana nodded and said she was going out for a walk. The boulevard they lived on was long and stretched all the way to the village of Marly. She knew she couldn't get lost—just walk straight in one direction, then turn around and walk back. She took an apple from the fruit bowl and tucked it into a large pocket in her jacket.

"I'll see you in a bit," she called as she shut the door.

Vowing to not even look in the windows of the patisseries that dotted the route, Diana walked briskly down the boulevard, smiling at the people she passed. The old men smiled and said, "*Bonjour, mademoiselle,*" and the older women seemed startled that she would even acknowledge them.

There was a shop selling sewing machines and another specializing in local cheeses. There was a Catholic church and a small grocery store, with posters in the windows advertising special prices on *jambon* and *saucissons*. As she rounded a bend in the road, she approached a bridge over the river. The river was far below her, and she paused to look down. *What a beautiful place this is*, she said to herself. *Whatever the future holds for me, I will appreciate the time I am here. But I need to land a job, and soon.*

She walked for another ten minutes before turning around and heading back to the apartment.

※

It was Monday afternoon, and Diana had no sooner entered the foyer of Pascale's home than she ran into the woman, standing next to an older, somewhat attractive man. *Ah, finally I get to meet her husband*, Diana thought. She smiled at them both.

"Oh, Diana! Hello," Pascale said. She looked so elegant, Diana noted, in crisp linen trousers the color of a wheat field, topped by a close-knit sweater of the prettiest blue. A wide gold bangle encircled her slender wrist and was matched by shiny gold ovals at her ears. Pascale's hair was sleek and smooth, like she had just walked out of a salon.

"Hello. How are you?" Diana smiled at the man. They made a good couple, she thought. Pascale might be more...elegant, but they were both attractive.

"Very well indeed, thanks. Diana, this is Monsieur Brusadin. You answered his ad for an *au pair*."

"Oh! Oh!" Not her husband then. This is Monsieur Brusadin. *Oh! I wish Mulligan were here.*

"Hah-lo," he said in a baritone voice. He extended his right hand, flashing a thick gold bracelet on his wrist. Unlike Pascale's jewelry, though, his was chain-link, heavy, and more suited for a man, if one were a man who favored bracelets, and clearly Monsieur Brusadin was such a man. "Nize due meet you." *He speaks English!* Diana was gratified, thinking that perhaps her lack of French fluency might not be a problem after all.

His shirt was open at the collar, and Diana spied more gold around his neck. His dark eyes raked her from head to toe, but his grin seemed more innocuous than lascivious. At least that was how Diana chose to interpret it. She guessed him to be about forty years old. He wore shiny brown shoes with pointed toes, and his trousers looked to be made of a kind of wrinkle-less fabric. *Disco lives on with this guy*, Diana thought.

"Do you like to drink coffee? There is a *patisserie* next door." His accent was Italian, even if his name wasn't. Still, he seemed to be classier than some of the guys she knew back home, in spite of the polyester pants. At least he wasn't wearing one of those nylon shirts with the long, pointed collar.

"Yes, of course. Thank you."

Pascale winked at Diana from behind Monsieur Brusadin's shoulder and mouthed 'good luck' before waving them off.

Monsieur Brusadin opened the door of the Sarine

Tea-Room, the very place Diana had drooled over every time she passed by. As he held the door open for her, she stepped inside ahead of him and breathed in the scent of buttery croissants and marzipan. He gestured to an empty table and held her chair until she sat. Within seconds, a uniformed server approached. "*Bonjour, m'sieur. M'mselle.*" The waitress focused solely on Monsieur Brusadin, as if Diana were invisible.

"Coffee for you?" Monsieur Brusadin asked Diana.

Diana nodded and Monsieur Brusadin ordered. An espresso for him and a '*café Americain*' for her. Then he said something else to the server that Diana didn't understand. The woman tilted her head as if she were a teenager, touched her graying hair, and giggled before turning away. Monsieur gave Diana a sizzling smile, big creamy-white teeth and a prominent overbite.

His medium-brown hair was longish in the back, falling over his collar, and Diana thought he might be trying to compensate for a receding hairline, because his hair was much thinner on top. His scalp and face were bronze, even in early May, and Diana guessed perhaps he worked outside, in the sun, all year long. The gold bracelet caught her eye again as he rested his hands on the table. When the waitress brought their coffees, he barely acknowledged her, and Diana watched the woman's face—a combination of disappointment and resentment, and Diana imagined Monsieur Brusadin had left many bruised hearts in his wake. Turn on the charm one minute, act as if they didn't exist the next. She knew a couple of guys like that. He dropped a cube of sugar into his cup and stirred it with a miniscule spoon.

The woman who had waited on them returned to the table and wordlessly set down a plate of assorted pastries, but Diana vowed not to take one unless he did. Fortunately, he pushed the plate toward her, saying, "Please, you choose first. Everything is good, I assure you."

"Thank you," she said, selecting a small tart filled with creamy custard. Monsieur Brusadin picked up a sugar-dusted oblong pastry.

"May I call you Diana?" He fixed his liquid brown eyes on her. Diana felt a flush creep up her neck, although she couldn't understand why.

"Of course." He didn't offer his own first name, so Diana assumed he wanted her to call him Monsieur Brusadin. *Well, sure*, she thought, *he's going to be my employer. Maybe.*

"My wife, she does not speak good English. You speak French, yes?"

"*Oui*," Diana replied. "A little. But I learn quickly."

Monsieur stroked his chin and laughed. "I am sure it will be fine. And I will be the translator." He set his dark eyes upon her again, until she looked down at her coffee. He unnerved her, although she couldn't say what it was that had her so disconcerted. He'd been very mannered with her, but it was the way he looked at her. She had had men ogle her before. Walter, the tennis instructor ten years her senior, who had attempted a quick feel as he showed her how to backhand volley. Ralph, the lifeguard at the beach club, who had invited her to sit with him high up in his lifeguard's chair at the end of his shift, then tried to untie her bathing suit top. Mr. Dorrance—oh god, Mr. Dorrance. She knew the look, and Monsieur Brusadin was giving her that look.

What kind of a situation is this, Diana asked herself. She didn't want a relationship with him. *Was that what he was thinking? Was it going to be like her father and Astrid?* If that were the case, she'd refuse the job. She wasn't there to fulfill some old guy's wacko fantasy.

"So," Diana ventured. "Can you tell me about the job?"

"Yes, of course. You will help my wife in the house to clean. Also help in the kitchen. Also to care for our child during the day because we are at work. You have...what is it...experience with children?"

"Yes. I like children," she said convincingly. "I have two younger brothers and I've done a lot of babysitting. Child care." She remembered babysitting for the Dorrance kids when she was seventeen. The Dorrances lived on Ocean Avenue, in a mansion they called Summersea. The children, Channing and Hutton, were well behaved and Mrs. Dorrance gave her fifty dollars for a few hours' work. It was great until that night Mr. Dorrance drove her home and pulled his Rolls-Royce off the road and into a dark dirt lot. He'd turned to face her, smelling of cigars and whiskey. He had a tan, even in November. Diana remembered the creases in his skin. He wasn't wearing his seat belt.

"How much does my wife pay you?" he had asked.

"She gave me fifty dollars tonight," Diana had answered. She waited for Mr. Dorrance to tell her that was too much. Her father had called Mr. Dorrance cheap more than once, even though he was probably a millionaire many times over. She half-expected him to ask for forty dollars back.

Instead, Mr. Dorrance leaned closer to her, so close his skin was almost right on hers. "I'll give you another hundred to take your top off—right now."

The area was dark, quiet. No houses, no streetlights, and it was after midnight. She could probably jump out of the car and run home. Was her door locked?

"No, Mr. Dorrance. Not now, not ever." Before she could open the car door, though, he'd grabbed her wrist and twisted her arm. "No," she said again, her voice cracking. With his other hand, he reached under her shirt and squeezed, so hard she cried out.

Her right hand was free, and she slapped his face, as hard as she could. Momentarily shocked, Mr. Dorrance grinned and said, "You want it rough? I'm all for rough, sweetheart," before grabbing her hair and pulling hard. Diana felt the pain from her scalp down her spine, but she wasn't going to let him have his way.

"Get the hell off me, you pervert," she grunted, pushing her thumb into one of his eyes. As he yelled, she pulled free, opened the car door, and ran as fast as she could until she'd reached the street where she lived. She kept turning her head to look behind her, in case he was following. But there were no headlights. *I hope I blinded the bastard.* Diana had stayed outside in the chilly November night air, hidden behind the house, for a long time before she finally crept inside and went upstairs to her room. Even then, in her bed, she could not stop trembling. What would she say? Mr. Dorrance would deny everything. *Was it my fault? Did I send out some kind of signal that I wanted him?* She didn't think so. But even remembering the encounter had brought back such painful memories that Diana felt her entire body tense.

Monsieur's words brought her back to the present, and she tossed her head to rid the memories. "You are American," he said. "What do you think of your president Reagan?" He leaned back in his chair and lifted his little espresso cup, holding it with his thumb and forefinger, like a dowager countess. Was he taunting her? Or was he genuinely interested in American politics?

"Well, I'm here, not there," Diana replied. Reagan might have been her father's choice, but she didn't care for him, with his cowboy outfits and his red cheeks. Like a cartoon character, he was. And his narrow, doting wife next to him. Diana had voted for Carter, but she had lied and assured her father she'd cast her vote for Reagan. He had congratulated her on her good sense and slipped her a twenty. "Go get yourself something, kitten," he'd said, laughing, as her mother turned away in disgust. Maybe her mother had voted for Carter, too.

Monsieur smiled easily. He set down his cup and

wiped his lips with a heavy paper napkin. Then he asked, "Why do Americans always say, 'We're number one'?"

Without pausing to consider her reply, Diana blurted, "Because we are." *Wait*, she thought, *are we?*

His thick eyebrows shot up. "Still, you are here," he said, jabbing the table with a long finger. His bracelet jingled. "Not there."

Diana lowered her chin. She had no witty come-back, no measured response. What could she say? Had she sounded like a stupid American with her response? Wasn't she supposed to feel that way? She and Mulligan had been discussing it the previous night, Mulligan telling her that some people in Switzerland, and in Europe, viewed Americans as arrogant, self-centered. "They have an impression that we think we're better than everyone else," she'd said. It had surprised Diana to think that people outside America might think less charitably about her country. Then again, Diana was not as well-versed in current affairs and global politics as she could be. The realization that America might not be 'number one' in the eyes of others was a surprise. *Maybe I've been living in a bubble*, she told herself. Did the Swiss think *they* were number one? Did the Italians? Monsieur was in Switzerland, not Italy. But she couldn't say that to him. She was interviewing for a job, after all.

Monsieur raised his hand to signal the waitress.

"Will you eat with my family this evening, Diana? I would like very much for you to meet my wife and my little boy."

"Yes, yes, thank you. *Merci*. So, I have the job?"

"Almost, Diana," he said, chuckling. "My wife is... uh...the boss. If she says yes, then it's okay." He made a circle with his thumb and index finger. "Okay?"

"Okay." Diana crossed her fingers under the table as Monsieur paid for the coffee and pastries. He pulled a small leather purse from his front pocket and paid the waitress, who handed him some coins in return. She no longer flirted with him the way she had done when he'd first sat down. The waitress asked Monsieur something, and when he nodded his assent, she took the plate of remaining pastries and brought it behind the counter. With a slight jerk of his head, Monsieur stood and walked to the counter, with Diana trailing behind him. Monsieur selected three more delicacies to add to the box. A different woman placed each piece on pink waxed paper, added the extra pieces from their plate, and laid them lovingly inside a pale pink box with a darker pink design on the lid. Then she tied the box with pink twine and presented the package to Monsieur, who accepted it and turned to Diana.

"I will return for you at six, yes?"

"Yes. Thank you, Monsieur. *Merci*."

"*Au revoir*, Diana."

ELEVEN

When Mulligan arrived back at the apartment from the university, Diana greeted her with a bear hug at the door.

"What? *What??* Is it your dad?"

"What? No. No, I don't know. Jeez, Mull. No, the guy for the babysitting job, he was here when I got back. He was talking to Pascale. Monsieur Brusadin. I don't know his first name. I call him Monsieur anyway. We talked about the job. He's picking me up at six so I can meet his wife and kid. Mull! I think I might get the job!"

"Hey, that's great. Really, Di. So, the interview went well? You liked him?"

"He's okay. Italian, but his English is pretty good. He said his wife doesn't speak a lot of English, but he'll translate. I was relieved, Mull. At least he speaks English!"

"Great! Well, go to their house and spend some time with them so you can find out and be sure. Get a good sense of things, you know? Watch them, and the boy."

"What should I wear?"

"Diana, it's not a cocktail party," Mulligan said,

laughing. "Dress normally, like you're going to lunch or something."

"This?" Diana held up a pair of soft gray slacks and a pink and gray cotton sweater patterned with triangles. She'd chosen the combination because it looked like something Lady Diana would wear.

"Yup. Perfect. With flats. And no perfume!"

❧

Precisely at six, Diana walked to the front door of Pascale's house and opened it, to find Monsieur Brusadin exiting a small green car. She didn't recognize the model or make, but it looked like a jellybean. Tiny.

"Hah-lo, Diana!"

"Hello, Monsieur. You're right on time."

"*Comme les Suisses*," he quipped. "You are ready?"

"Yes," she said, folding herself into the little car.

Monsieur sped up the boulevard, then swung a hard right onto Route Neuve. Diana watched out the window as the town blurred by.

As he took another sharp turn, she was suddenly pressed against his right arm and realized she'd never fastened her seat belt. She grabbed it and buckled up.

"Okay?" he asked, never taking his eyes off the winding road.

"Yes," she gasped. The scenery was unfamiliar, and Diana assumed they were on the outskirts of the town. Stacks of tall gray-and-white apartment buildings stood in the hills to her right, but they were gone in an instant, as Monsieur shifted gears. Diana drew her knees away from the gear shaft. Would he try to cop a feel at sixty miles an hour? *They're not all like that, Diana*, she told herself, and tried to relax.

As they crested a hill, a farm came into view. The land stretched before her in shades of brown and green. A russet-roofed barn stood, with its upper story jutting out over the first level, and a ramp led from the ground up to the jutted-out upper story. A short distance away was a farmhouse, its ground-level floor made of stone. The upper two stories were dark brown, with sea-green shutters at the windows. Window boxes held red geraniums, in early bloom. As Monsieur rounded the final bend, Diana spotted a much smaller house, a white one-level cottage, that sat on the edge of the property.

Monsieur turned left into an unpaved driveway. Gravel kicked up and rattled the undercarriage of the tiny car. He cursed at the chickens that clawed at the dirt and scattered at the very last moment.

"One day I will kill one of these chickens and we will eat it," he snarled. Then he turned to Diana and laughed, baring his big white teeth.

He pulled around to the side of the house and slowed as the car edged down a slight incline. He set the brake and turned off the motor.

"*Voila!* We are here," he said, using his hands to show off the scene in front of her.

Diana tried to steady her heart rate as she extricated

herself from the car. With dismay, she realized she should have brought flowers for Madame Brusadin. But with what? She had no money, and there were no flowers growing outside of Pascale's apartment.

Monsieur led the way up steep stone steps to the front door. He turned a long brass handle down and pushed the door open, gesturing for Diana to enter first.

Diana wiped her feet thoroughly on the mat and entered a small, dark foyer.

"Anne-Marie? *On est là,*" Monsieur called from behind her.

"*Oui, j'arrive.*" Within seconds, a blonde woman appeared, wiping her hands on a white cotton apron. She looked to be in her late thirties. Her blonde bob was parted in the middle and she had wispy bangs on her forehead. Her dark eyebrows were tweezed thin and arched high, giving her a look of perpetual surprise. Her thin lips curved upward in a smile as she rested her dark eyes on Diana.

"This is Diana," Monsieur said, with his hand resting on his wife's shoulder. She pulled away from under it and extended her hand.

"Hah-lo," she said carefully. The look in her eyes, what was it, Diana wondered. Perhaps a mix of fear and anxiety and hopefulness?

Diana took her hand. It was thin and damp, in spite of her having wiped it on her apron. Diana smiled back.

"*Bonjour,*" she said, keeping the promise she had made earlier that she would try to speak French, even if it came out all wrong. "*Je suis heureuse de faire votre connaissance.*" I am happy to make your acquaintance. Mulligan had made her practice the sentence until she had it right. Diana felt like Audrey Hepburn in *My Fair Lady*, perfecting the line about the rain in Spain.

Madame smiled broadly, showing a gap between her two front teeth. "*Et toi aussi, Diana. Viens.* Well-come."

Diana followed Madame through the kitchen, a small but functional space with smaller and narrower appliances than Diana was accustomed to seeing. A small four-burner stove and a refrigerator that was half the size of the one that stood in the Driscolls' kitchen in Newport. She spied a large wooden bowl full of greens on a counter.

Monsieur reappeared with a small boy in his arms.

"And this is Kenny."

Kenny! What an odd name for a Swiss boy, Diana thought. Or was it? Was his name Kenneth?

"Kenny, *salut.*" She looked into the boy's face. So perfect in its baby-ness. Plump cheeks, a button of a nose, a pouty lower lip. He had a full head of hair, all dark curls, and those eyelashes! Diana felt her heart swell inside her chest. The sight of Kenny brought to mind her younger brothers, Chip and Cam, and she was filled with love and sadness at their current situation. She smiled at Kenny.

At that moment, Kenny let out an ear-piercing shriek.

"*Non!*" he yelled, pointing a tiny finger at Diana. "*Non! Non! Non!*"

"Kenny," Monsieur shushed. He turned to Diana. "I speak French and English to him. And I speak even Italian sometimes, more so when he makes me angry. He'll grow up speaking three languages," he added, beaming as the child squirmed in his arms, eager to escape the confines of his father's embrace.

But he must be so confused. Diana's unspoken thought troubled her. She smiled at the boy again, feeling a strange, unknown connection to him. *Why did he seem so familiar?* He looked nothing like her golden-haired brothers. Was it the maternal pull that all women were supposed to feel? Diana had no wish to birth children, at least not for a while. No, it wasn't that.

"Kenny," she murmured. "Is it Kenneth, Monsieur?"

"What? Kenneth?" Monsieur had a hard time with the 'th' sound, so it came out as 'Kennet.'

"Is Kenny short for Kenneth?"

Monsieur looked puzzled. "No, it's Kenny. Like Kenny Rogers." *Ken-nee Raj-err.* Monsieur grinned and sang, "You gots to know win to hole 'em, know win to fole 'em."

"Oh," Diana stuttered. *Oh my god*, she thought. *He's named Kenny because Monsieur likes "The Gambler" song. Wait until I tell Mulligan.*

"Anne? We eat now?"

"*Oui, oui.*" Diana heard a lot of noise in the kitchen and stepped to the doorway.

"Can I help? Um, *puis-je vous aider*?" she asked Madame, whose name she now knew was Anne-Marie.

But, like Monsieur, whose first name she still did not know, she would call them Madame and Monsieur.

"*Merci*, Diana." Madame handed her the bowl of salad to place on the table, then, using thick oven mitts, she withdrew a bubbling casserole from the oven and set it on top of the stove.

"*Assieds-toi, s'il te plaît*," she whispered, as Monsieur set Kenny into his highchair. Please sit.

Diana avoided eye contact with the boy, fearful she'd set him off again. Clearly, he didn't want her in the house. The question was, who would make the decision about whether she got the job or not, Madame and Monsieur? Or little Kenny, named after Kenny Rogers?

All attempts at conversation during dinner were interrupted by Kenny, who demanded his parents' attention and screamed if either of them turned their attention to Diana. Madame focused her efforts on feeding the boy as her own dinner grew cold.

Monsieur refilled his wine glass and held the bottle aloft over Diana's.

"Diana? More wine for you?" He stared at her intently until she felt the same uneasiness. He might not have intended it, but his look was so...brazen. So alpha-male. She hadn't been with a man in months, and maybe she'd forgotten what flirting was like. Not that she would flirt with Monsieur in any event, but especially not with his wife sitting across the table. She didn't flirt with married men. No, she recognized that look. She'd seen it too many times. And his wife was sitting right there. Monsieur ignored both his wife and his son as he poured wine into Diana's glass. Men like Monsieur needed to feel desired. He was probably about forty years old, but he needed someone young, like Diana, to assure him he was still attractive. *Maybe the connection between Madame and Monsieur isn't there anymore,* Diana thought. A warning bell went off in her head.

"Just half, please," she stammered. He filled the glass anyway. It was good wine. Even if they didn't offer her the job, at least she'd had a good meal and wine, excellent wine. But the little boy—Kenny!—hated her. Why in the world would they hire her if the boy hated her? And did she want the job? *I need a job. I need to earn money somehow,* she reminded herself.

Kenny had had enough. Diana glanced at Madame's plate, her food barely touched. Would Monsieur offer to put the boy to bed, just so Madame could eat? Kenny demanded to be released from the prison of his highchair. His cries grew louder as both parents attempted to ignore him, until no one could speak or hear each other.

Madame sat glumly, moving food around on her plate with her fork as Monsieur emptied his wine glass and wiped the corner of his mouth with his napkin.

When Kenny's screams could no longer be tolerated, Monsieur glared at Madame and lifted his son from his chair. He set Kenny on the floor, where Kenny continued his tantrum, lying on his stomach and kicking his little legs in the air. And screaming. Non-stop screaming. Diana could feel a headache starting.

"He did not have a sleep today," Monsieur told Diana, with a shrug and a 'what-can-you-do?' expression on his face. "But he is a good boy. When he sleeps during the day, he is very good."

"Of course," Diana said. "Poor thing, he's exhausted." Diana turned to Madame. "*Pauvre bébé; il est fatigué.*" Diana smiled at her triumph of the language, then nodded sympathetically to Madame.

Madame nodded and grasped Diana's hand, squeezing it so tightly Diana winced. "*Oui*, Diana. *Merci.* Sank you." She stood and picked up Diana's empty plate.

"Oh, I'll help." Diana stood as well, gathering plates and silverware. She swayed a little on her feet from the very good wine. Monsieur picked up the empty bottle and held it out to Diana.

"*Merci*, Diana," he said. He sat at the table as Madame and Diana cleared the table. Kenny lay quietly on the floor at Monsieur's feet. Perhaps he realized the show was over, or perhaps he'd screamed himself to sleep. Diana couldn't tell.

In the kitchen, Madame rinsed the plates and stacked them in the sink, then covered the casserole with aluminum foil and slid it into the narrow refrigerator.

She held a finger to her lips and signaled Diana to follow her back to the dining room, where Kenny still lay on the floor, now sound asleep. Monsieur had moved to the sofa in the adjoining living room, shoeless feet up and one arm over his eyes. Diana felt she shouldn't allow him to drive her back to Mulligan's apartment, not in his present state. He had drunk most of the bottle of very good wine and had apparently poured himself a glass of brandy, as the empty glass and bottle sat on the cleared table. She would have to telephone Pascale and ask her to come out to the little white house at the edge of the farm. Or perhaps Madame could drive her back.

Madame lifted Kenny into her arms. He opened heavy-lidded eyes for an instant, then dropped his head onto her shoulder and fell back asleep. Diana followed them down the hallway to Kenny's room. The walls were painted sky blue, and the furniture was white. Madame lowered Kenny to a changing table and gently undressed him, putting on a clean diaper. She slid his limbs into cotton pajamas and buttoned them up as he slept. Diana checked her watch. It was half past seven, and still light out. Should he be put down this early? Would he end up waking at four in the morning? Diana had no idea, but she could understand why Madame wanted to put him to bed.

Madame transferred Kenny to his crib, covered him with a pale blue blanket and leaned down low to kiss his forehead. She turned on a dim nightlight and pulled the door over, leaving it ajar by an inch.

"*Il est mignon,*" Diana whispered when they were back in the hallway. He's cute.

"*Oui, quand il dort,*" Madame said with a little laugh. Yes, when he sleeps.

They returned to the living room, and Madame gently shook Monsieur's shoulder until he woke. At first he looked at her like he had never seen his own wife before, then he sat up and yawned. He raked a hand through his hair and looked at Diana.

"Ah," he said. "Yes, yes." He blinked hard and gave his cheek a hard slap.

With a quick glance to his wife, who nodded, he turned to Diana.

"Diana, my wife and I will like very much to offer you the job, as our *au pair*. Do you like to work for us this summer?"

A job! She'd have a job! And money! Mulligan was right, she could only deal with what was in front of her. A thousand thoughts fluttered through her mind— what would happen with her father, would she be able to go to London for the royal wedding? How much would they pay her? *Focus, Diana.* Here was a job offer. And money. Bird in the hand and all that. The Eccell Institute job was not likely to happen, and here she could work, get some money. Hopefully everything with her father would get straightened out in time for her to still get to London by the end of July.

"Yes. *Oui*," Diana said directly to Madame, who clasped her hands together in supplication.

"Very good. Sank you," Monsieur said. He looked again at his wife. "So. You will have your own room and eat with us, yes, and we pay you one hundred francs each month. You will start on the first day of June unless you wish to move in now?" He pushed his hair back from his high, tan forehead. "Did my wife show you your room?"

Wait. Wait, what? I'm going to live *with them? Was that in the ad?* Diana frowned, and tried to remember. Of course, where would she live after Mulligan left to go home? Diana didn't even know if Pascale would rent the apartment to her, and of course she wouldn't make enough money from the job to pay rent and buy food. Of course not. A hundred francs a month! Her father had asked Diana to keep her spending under five hundred dollars a month when he handed her the American Express card, and five hundred dollars was almost a thousand Swiss francs. Ten times what Monsieur Brusadin was offering. *Oh my god*, she said to herself. Her insides coiled tightly, veins and arteries and intestines all wrapped around each other, cutting off oxygen and her blood supply. Her father's American Express card was no good. She didn't have a thousand francs a month. She had two francs and thirty centimes and she'd still need a loan from Mulligan until she got paid.

"Diana?" Monsieur's voice broke into her thoughts.

She blinked hard. This was being an adult then, having responsibility for herself. A hard reality enveloped her like a thick, choking fog. She fought back tears.

"Yes. *Oui*. I accept the job." Her head felt as if it weighed a thousand pounds.

When Monsieur stood to take Diana back to Fribourg, she didn't even consider whether he was sober enough to drive. Or maybe she didn't care.

TWELVE

Mulligan was waiting when Diana arrived back at the apartment. Diana saw her expectant face and knew she should be more relieved, or even more excited. After all, she had a job. And she would have a little money. A reason to stay, and not go home to face the awful matter of her father in jail. But a hundred francs a month? Even if she didn't spend one centime all summer, she still wouldn't have enough for an airline ticket back to the States.

"Well?" Mulligan's hands flapped at her sides.

"Well, they offered me a job. And I said yes." Diana dropped into one of the chairs, more exhausted than she realized. Her gut had stayed clenched as Monsieur drove back to town, and only once she was slumped in the chair did she allow herself to fill her lungs with air.

"That's great! Diana, this is fantastic news. Tell me about the family." Mulligan's excitement was so evident, Diana reminded herself to be gracious about the situation.

"Well, first of all, I'm going to live with them. I have to. The job includes room and board."

"Okay, that's okay. This way you don't need to think about rent and groceries. That's a good thing." Mulligan's face looked so positive, so relieved.

Diana would not mention the hundred francs a month, not yet. "Right."

"And the little boy?"

"Cute." Diana described Kenny's features. "Really, he's adorable. But he threw a temper tantrum during dinner. That was not a pretty sight." Diana shook her head, remembering Kenny's hysterics.

Mulligan chuckled. "Be glad there's just one kid then."

"Yeah. Well, the parents are kind of old, so I don't think there'll be any more kids."

Mulligan paused. "How old?"

Diana shrugged. "I don't know, kind of old for a two-year-old, late thirties, I'm thinking. He might even be forty." She rolled her eyes. "He was right out of central casting, Mull. Like an aging Casanova. He's Italian, even though his name doesn't sound Italian. The open-collar shirt, the gold chains." She laughed at the memory of Monsieur and her first impressions.

"What do you mean? Describe him." Mulligan sat forward, her elbows resting on her knees.

"Remember that time we went to Little Italy? Remember those two guys who wanted to buy us dinner? The gold chains, the pinky rings, the tans? Like that. He reminded me of one of those guys. I mean, I think he's harmless, but he can't look at me without checking me out at the same time." Diana gave a little shimmy in disgust and imitated Monsieur, giving Mulligan the once-over.

"Hold on, Di. What about the mom? Describe her."

"Okay, well, her name is Anne-Marie, or Anne. I don't know his first name, though. He's just Monsieur, she's Madame, I guess that's how they want it. Oh! And get this. The kid? His name is Kenny. *Kenny!* Not Kenneth. I asked Monsieur about it and he told me they named him after Kenny Rogers! Because Monsieur likes 'The Gambler.' He even sang a couple of lines from the song. Oh my god, Mull, it was all I could do to keep from laughing. I mean, isn't that hilarious?"

"Diana, what does the mom *look* like?"

"Oh. Well, late thirties, I'm guessing, like I said. Blonde. Bleached blonde, I'm pretty sure. Straight hair, like in a bob. Not really pretty but that's mean, because she was very nice. Her nose is kind of like a beak, you know? Thin lips. She just doesn't smile very much. Oh, a little gap between her front teeth. She seemed self-conscious about it, but it's not bad. And they both smoke. Ugh. But what could I say? At least the windows were open."

"Diana."

"What? What's wrong?"

"Remember a while back when we were at the Plaza café? Remember the kid who ran into the street and was almost hit by a car? *Remember?*"

Diana stared at her friend. She willed her mind to go

back to that warm, sunny afternoon. The screech of the brakes. The yelling. Everyone standing to get a better look. Diana's view blocked, Mulligan describing it.

"A little kid ran into the street and almost got hit by a car. Yeah, I remember you telling me. I didn't see it."

"And remember I described the parents? I thought they could even be grandparents? Smoking? You just described those people."

"Oh," Diana said, as the air left her lungs. "Oh, Mull. I never saw them."

"I know, but the way you described them, I'd bet money on it. The kid. Dark curly hair, right?"

Diana nodded. She remembered Mulligan describing the parents, or grandparents, as being so cavalier about the incident. Mulligan outraged that they weren't paying attention and let their child, or grandchild, wander into a busy road. No wonder she'd had a strange sensation about him. The little boy, weaving in and out of the café tables. Dark curly hair.

"Remember I made a crack about the guy and the gold chain around his neck?"

"I didn't remember until just now," Diana mumbled. She looked up. "Did I just make a huge mistake?"

Mulligan sprang to her feet and pasted a smile on her face. "Listen, I'm sure everything will be fine. You got a job! That's terrific. I'll take you out tomorrow to celebrate."

Diana didn't move from her chair. Her shoulders sagged, as if there was a two-year-old boy straddling them.

"I should have waited before saying yes," she said. "The fancy boarding school could still come through, and it pays really well." Diana swiped at a tear, angry that she was about to cry. "That job pays two thousand francs for the summer." She looked up at her friend. "Mull. This job pays a *hundred* francs a *month*. Not even enough to pay you back. Not enough to fly home, if I even wanted to. And the wedding in London?" She blew out a ragged sigh. "Looks like that's out. My life officially sucks."

"Hey, stop." Mulligan sat down opposite her.

"Oh, and the kid hates me. I should have mentioned that." Diana wrapped her arms around her chest, as if a cold breeze had suddenly cut through her. "I'm officially a loser."

"Diana, you have never thought of yourself as a loser, and you're not going to start now. Okay, your father was arrested. Your money supply—your very *generous* money supply—has been cut off. How does that make you a loser? Your father, if he's guilty, he's the loser. Not Diana Enid Driscoll."

"Yeah, okay. Thanks, Mull. But life right now is about as crappy as it can be."

"Stop it," Mulligan said sharply. "You are here, and I'm happy about that. You don't know what tomorrow is going to bring."

"I'm still hoping to get the Eccell Institute job," Diana said. "If they offer it to me, I'll just tell Monsieur that I got a better offer."

"You already told them yes, though, right?"

"Yeah, but..."

"Diana."

"Oh, for god's sake, Mull, do you always have to be so ethical?"

❧

Diana sent a letter home, to her Newport address, even though her mother and the boys were up in Providence. Her mother would either go back for the mail or it would be forwarded. What about school for Chip and Cam? Diana couldn't worry about that; it was out of her control, and the current school year was nearly finished, anyway. What was that prayer her mother used to say? *Serenity to accept the things I cannot change?* Something like that.

The following day, before she even had a chance to get her hopes up for the Eccell Institute job, Mulligan's friend Pam told her that an American student named Gina had gotten the job, and was going to teach disco dancing to the little princes and princesses. Disco dancing!

Okay then, Diana. She lifted her chin and told herself to let it go. *My new chapter begins June first.* Whatever was to be, she would accept it. There still might be a way to get to London for the wedding. Her father's situation might be rectified. *Never stop hoping, Diana.*

THIRTEEN

Kenny was wary around Diana, but by the beginning of her second week, he was snuggling up next to her, sleepy-eyed, with the ever-present binky in his mouth. As he fell into a deep sleep, Diana carefully moved away from him on the sofa, then pushed cushions around him and put more on the floor, in case he rolled off. She felt as if she should never take her eyes off him, even when he was sleeping. She had made the mistake a few days ago of trying to lift him and bring him to his crib, but he woke up and started howling, so she figured it was better if he just napped on the sofa. As long as he didn't roll off.

It was quarter to three in the afternoon and Diana had cleaned up after the big noontime meal. She washed and dried the dishes, put everything back where it belonged (Madame was very particular about things being in a certain place), and wiped down the kitchen to Madame's exacting specifications. Monsieur and Madame arrived home each day at ten past noon, and they left to go back to work shortly before two o'clock, to return home for the day shortly before six, except on the days that Monsieur's schedule involved leaving the house later. When Kenny behaved during a meal, it was as if they all lived in a perfect world. But that was not the typical day, Diana soon understood.

Kenny was generally good in the morning. Perhaps the reality of his day without his parents, with just Diana, hadn't yet hit him. Diana rose at six each morning, as did Madame. Together they prepared for the day ahead, in a sort of silent dance that Diana learned quickly. Madame washed and dressed while Diana, who bathed in the evening, slipped off the long t-shirt she slept in and pulled on her usual 'uniform' of khaki slacks and a cotton shirt. She finger-combed her Lady Di haircut and slipped into the bathroom as soon as she heard Madame emerge, brushing her teeth and making a quick toilet.

They met up in the kitchen, where a typed sheet was pinned to a square of corkboard on a wall. The sheet listed a week's worth of meals (*Lundi—salade Niçoise*) and what was expected of Diana prior to Monsieur and Madame's arrival for the midday meal. Madame posted a fresh sheet each Sunday night, ready for a new, carefully controlled week ahead.

Mardi—Omelette aux herbes avec salade verte
Diana—preparer la salade

Since it was Tuesday, Diana's assignment was to make the salad ahead of time, just before they arrived home at noon, and Madame would make the omelet. There was a wooden bowl on the counter. Diana was instructed to whisk the salad dressing first in the bowl: olive oil, white vinegar, Maggi seasoning, Dijon mustard, and salt and pepper. Madame was specific in the proportions, and had watched Diana closely the first time she made the dressing. The olive oil stood next to the wooden bowl, a tall, thin bottle with a silver dispenser top that Diana had seen on liquor bottles. The vinegar was in a cut-glass cruet with a glass stopper. The Maggi seasoning came in a bright red-and-yellow canister, and required 'four to six' shakes, and the Dijon mustard was in a jar that looked as if it was filled with yellow and brown seeds. It was pungent and so different from the French's mustard Diana enjoyed on a hot dog.

Once Madame and Diana were dressed and together in the kitchen, Madame prepared coffee in a silver pot on the stove. She had taught Diana how to make coffee, because Monsieur and Madame drank coffee in the morning and again at noon. Diana enjoyed one cup in the morning, but found the strong, bitter coffee made her too jittery throughout the rest of the day. She imagined Madame and Monsieur needed it after drinking so much wine at the midday meal.

The hexagonal pot had a hinged lid. Madame spooned coarse ground coffee into the basket and leveled it off. She used hot water to fill the bottom part of the pot right up close to the limit. Then she placed the coffee basket into the bottom part and screwed on the top part. She set the pot on the stove. As the heat brought the hot water to a boil, the pressure pushed the coffee up into the top part of the pot. Madame made sure Diana understood to listen for the bubbling noise, because that was when she had to take the pot off the stove. Recalling the Mister Coffee coffeemaker at their home in Newport, Diana appreciated how it was so much easier—add water, put in filter, spoon in coffee, push a button.

Perhaps Madame's need for such precision and repetitive acts was her way to keep control in the house, Diana guessed. She'd never encountered anyone so methodical, and so insistent on the exact way of doing things. The previous weekend, she had discussed it with Mulligan, who surmised that Madame's need to control her kitchen might stem from anxiety. "Anxiety?" Diana had asked. "I don't know about that. She doesn't seem anxious." Mulligan had countered, "Maybe it's because she has these habits. Think about it, Diana. She works as a secretary, right? So she gets bossed around at work. You've said the situation at home isn't all that great. Maybe the only thing she can control is the kitchen—and you."

Diana filled a small cup for Madame and one for herself. Madame drank her coffee black, but Diana needed a spoonful of sugar and a dash of cream in hers. They sipped the first cup in comfortable silence while Monsieur and Kenny slept, and Diana understood how important that early quiet was to Madame, as she'd come to treasure it, too. Even if it was just an hour. Outside, a barn swallow sang until another joined in. The morning breeze through the open window was fresh, tinged with the smells of the farm—grass, manure, the earth.

Madame didn't eat breakfast, but after a second cup of coffee, she rose from the table and returned to her bedroom to dress, and presumably, to wake Monsieur.

Monsieur generally emerged from his bedroom around seven, bare-chested and barefoot, in light-colored pajama bottoms. His chest was broad, with a smattering of dark and gray curly hair across it, hair that trailed down his stomach in a thin line. Diana usually looked away, as she didn't want to even think about that trail of hair and where it ended. On someone else, maybe, but not Monsieur. After running into him once outside the bathroom, Diana had tried to remain in the kitchen, listening to his movements as he prepared for his day ahead. Diana would hear him in the bathroom, and when he entered the dining room, Monsieur was, for the most part, genial. He was comfortable walking around the house in just his pajama bottoms, even though Diana had heard Madame tell him to get himself dressed before he walked into other parts of the house. He had responded to her once that it was his house. Diana listened and tried to understand their conversation. It *was* his house, after all, and she'd seen her father do the same. As long as Monsieur kept to himself, he could preen about the house, with his developed pecs and chest hair, all he wanted.

Monsieur drank one small cup of coffee standing up, usually looking out the window at the farm. What was he thinking? That he would rather be a farmer? Did he come from a long line of Italian farmers? Diana knew practically nothing about him. Sometimes he sang softly, as if to himself, a tune with Italian lyrics that she couldn't begin to understand.

Madame had asked Diana not to wake Kenny until she and Monsieur had left the house, precisely at seven-forty-five each morning. Diana complied, of course, but wondered why. She found out one day when Kenny awakened early. Calling out *maman* and *papa* over and over again, Monsieur finally strode into the boy's room to get him up. Madame was applying black eyeliner at the table in the dining room, using a compact mirror. She muttered something under her breath, then apologized to Diana, even though Diana didn't hear what she'd said.

"Ce ne sera pas facile," she said, grimacing first at Diana and then, looking in the mirror, at the imperfect line drawn on her eyelid. *This won't be easy.* Diana shook her head, not understanding. But as soon as Madame and Monsieur said goodbye and left the house, Kenny let out a wail that could have been heard seven kilometers away in Granges-Paccot. It took Diana nearly fifteen minutes to calm the boy, who had most likely exhausted himself with his sobbing.

With Kenny placated, or rather bribed with a couple of Frey Petit-Buerre cookies, Diana took a thick slice of bread from the breadbox. She slathered it with silky butter and apricot preserves, or, once in a while, Nutella, a creamy chocolate-hazelnut spread that was so decadent Diana couldn't imagine why it wasn't popular in America. She could fill a suitcase with the jars. Chip and Cam would be in heaven. She shared bits of bread with Kenny, knowing Madame would have disapproved of the decidedly sugary breakfast her son had just enjoyed. She hoped it wouldn't become a habit, and wondered if Madame had yelled at Monsieur on the drive into town.

The following morning, Monsieur seemed to have learned his lesson, and thankfully, Kenny was sleeping, or at least quiet, in his room. Madame prepared to leave the house, but in response to Diana's questioning expression, she explained that Monsieur would be picked up at nine by his co-worker Luigi. Diana nodded her understanding, but stayed away from the bread and Nutella while Monsieur was around. She knew it shouldn't matter, that she had every right to eat breakfast. But Monsieur was the kind of guy who might say something, like *"Attention! Tu vas grossir!"* Careful, you'll get fat! Like it was any of his business what she ate.

The house was quiet. Monsieur might still be asleep, Diana thought, and perhaps would not want to be wakened by his own son. But then again, she had a job to do. Diana tiptoed into Kenny's room to wake him gently. On many days, he was already awake, his big brown eyes following her around the room, as she lifted the shade at the window, cooed a good morning to him. By not seeing his mother in the morning, and by not seeing her leave the house, Kenny seemed unaware that she was even missing. But at least he didn't pitch a fit.

"*Bonjour*, Kenny, *bonjour*," she said, touching the boy's head. Kenny didn't say much, and Diana wondered if all the different languages confused him. She tried not to speak English in front of him unless she was very mad. The poor little kid, he looked lost. How many *au pair* girls had lived here? How many had walked away?

While she was in Kenny's room and changing him, she heard Monsieur moving about the house, humming to himself. Diana hesitated, unsure as to whether she should carry Kenny out to see his father, who was probably leaving soon. She played with him a little longer, softly cooing his name and the few French words she could think of. He was docile and happy, and she felt a pull to the little boy that startled her.

The dilemma of whether to bring Kenny out didn't matter, because Diana heard a car on the gravel drive beneath Kenny's window. Resting Kenny on her hip, she peeked out to see a dark blue Volkswagen with an indistinguishable person behind the wheel. That must be Monsieur's friend Luigi, Diana thought. But then she heard laughter, and one of the voices belonged to a woman. She peeked out again to see a pretty woman with wavy dark hair exit from the driver's seat. She tossed her hair and laughed again.

"Who is that?" Diana whispered, keeping Kenny

away from the window. She made sure to stay hidden as she watched the woman circle the car to the passenger side, touching Monsieur's arm as they passed. Monsieur slipped into the driver's seat and backed the car out of the gravel driveway before speeding off.

"Not Luigi, that's for sure," she said out loud.

Monsieur had told Diana that he and Luigi sold insurance, that there were a lot of Italians who worked in Switzerland, people who only trusted other Italians. Diana thought that perhaps Monsieur and Luigi let these people believe that the Swiss were less trustworthy. Or maybe they all spoke Italian. Was that woman a client? Another Italian co-worker? *I don't think I want to know*, she thought.

❧

One afternoon, while Kenny slept on the sofa next to her, Diana opened a paperback book that Mulligan had given to her. It was a steamy romance novel that pushed the boundaries. A takeoff on *Lolita*, the book revolved around an aging chemistry professor and his nubile young student. The sex scenes were as graphic as any Diana had ever read, and she hid the book from Madame and Monsieur, even though Madame wouldn't be able to understand it.

God, I miss sex, Diana thought. *Not that there have been that many, only two before Myles, and they were not memorable.* She was hoping for a torrid affair, either in

Switzerland or in London, but there hadn't been any opportunities. It wasn't like she could ask Madame, or even Pascale, to fix her up. Mulligan didn't seem interested in dating anyone, especially since she only had a couple of weeks left before she headed home. When Diana had asked, Mulligan scoffed and told her she had spent her time concentrating on her classwork. "But what about fun, Mull?" Diana had asked. "We're young, we're cute. Surely there must be a couple of Swiss boys who would want to take us out?" Actually, Diana thought, it might be better to find an older Swiss man. Or was the novel getting to her? No, she'd rather be with someone more mature, more established. Just not as old as her father. Or Monsieur.

The house was quiet, but Diana didn't want to play the radio and risk waking Kenny. One station played American popular music, and Diana was content to stay current with the latest hits. She swatted away a fly. Madame hated the flies. She said there were so many because the house sat on the edge of the farm, and the flies were drawn to the cows, and the cows' *merde*. Diana thought perhaps having screens in the windows would be a solution, but she didn't know how to make the suggestion. Were screens not common? And why not? Of course there would be flies if there were no screens in the windows!

She rose quietly, glancing at Kenny, who sucked on his binky as he slept. In the kitchen, she opened a cupboard and found a bar of chocolate, studded with whole hazelnuts. Just one square, she told herself. They wouldn't mind—after all, the job included room and board. *This is board. I'm entitled to a snack*, she thought, even as it passed through her mind that she should purchase chocolate and stash it in her room.

Ten minutes later the entire bar of chocolate was gone and Diana knew she'd have to replace it. But how? The house was surrounded by the farm, and the nearest market was at least a twenty-minute walk away. And she couldn't leave Kenny.

"Crap." Diana paced the floor. Was there any other chocolate in the house, in case Madame or Monsieur, more likely Monsieur, had a craving? She couldn't tell him that she'd just eaten an entire bar of chocolate. He would look her up and down and make another comment about the dangers of getting fat. She wasn't fat, but she wasn't as diligent as Madame about her eating, either. Maybe he'd threatened to leave Madame if she got fat. *And who was that woman who picked him up?* Diana stashed the chocolate's wrapper in her room, vowing to replace the bar at her next opportunity.

Mulligan had lent Diana fifty francs, to tide her over until she got paid, which was mid-month. Diana owed Mulligan a total of ninety francs, not even counting the lunches and dinners Mull had paid for. Ninety francs seemed like very little when she had free access to the credit card, but now? It was a daunting amount. Nearly a month's pay.

She still hadn't heard from her mother, even though

Diana had sent her a letter with the Brusadins' address and telephone number. Was she angry at Diana for deciding to stay? She tried to understand her mother's fear of an uncertain future, even as she remained convinced that the situation with her father was a misunderstanding. Her father wasn't a criminal! Still, she hoped to hear from her mother, just to let Diana know what was happening at home. Before she had moved into the Brusadins' house in Düdingen, she'd told Mulligan everything she knew about her father's arrest. Mulligan had listened quietly, without offering any advice or judgement. She was empathetic, as any good friend would be, and agreed with Diana that perhaps the feds had gotten it all wrong.

As Kenny slept, Diana picked up the telephone receiver. She dialed Pascale's number and waited.

"Diana! It's good to hear your voice. How is everything going for you?"

"It's fine, Pascale, thank you. I'm doing all right. Is Mulligan around, by any chance?" Kenny murmured in his sleep, but didn't wake.

"Yes, she's here. I will go get her." Diana listened as Pascale's footsteps faded away, then she heard a door close and pictured Pascale walking briskly down the hallway to knock on Mulligan's door. She waited, heard the door open again and then Mulligan's voice on the phone.

"Hey, Di. You okay?"

"Yeah. Kenny's sleeping. I just wanted to hear your voice. It's so quiet here."

"Aw, I can imagine. Are you adjusting, though? Are they nice to you?"

"Yeah, they're okay. He's still a little creepy, but he hasn't done anything. I don't think he would, if I'm being honest. So, I ate an entire bar of chocolate a few minutes ago."

She heard Mulligan laugh on the other end. "So what? They're supposed to feed you. They'll get more. Was it the only bar of chocolate in the house?"

"No, there's another one that has bits of wheat in it. Ugh. Hey, Mull, listen. I haven't heard from my mother, even though she has my new address and phone number. I'm going out of my mind here wondering. Do you think you could ask your father to see if he can find out what's going on?"

Mulligan's silence on the other end had a swarm of anxious bees buzzing inside Diana's brain.

"Do you know anything, Mull? Is there something you're not telling me? I have to know, whatever it is."

"No. I haven't asked. But I will. I'm calling home tomorrow to confirm my flight back. I'll ask him what he knows, I'll tell him you're concerned."

"I'm so sad you're leaving. I wish you could stay a little longer."

"We'll see each other on Sunday, Diana."

"My work week ends at noon on Saturday. Could I come stay with you Saturday night?"

"Sure. You can stay every weekend for as long as I'm here. I'll see you Saturday."

❧

Saturday morning Diana cleaned the house with Madame. Madame showed her the 'proper' way to clean, and it was intense. Was this how Nydia cleaned the house in Newport? Diana took care of her own bedroom—making her bed, hanging her clothes, dusting her bureau, but Kenny's furniture was wiped and disinfected, everything in the main bathroom was scrubbed—bathtub, sink, toilet, toothbrush holder, the kitchen floor mopped. Cupboards wiped, rugs vacuumed, windows washed. By ten minutes to noon, they were finished, and Diana was coated in sweat. Madame flopped on the sofa and waved her hand at Diana to do the same. But Diana couldn't wait to head into town.

In halting French, she told Madame that she was going to stay with her friend until Sunday evening.

"*Un ami ou une amie?*" she asked. A male friend or a female friend? Diana felt her cheeks grow warm.

"*Une amie. Une femme,*" she replied.

"*Bon. Attention aux jeunes hommes,*" Madame murmured. Watch out for young men.

Diana laughed and returned to her bedroom for her overnight bag. Young men. And older men, she should have added. Calling goodbye again, she let herself out the door and turned onto the road, the Route de Berne. The road led to Fribourg, but Diana wondered if walking in the other direction would take her to Bern? How long would that take? The day that she and Mulligan had taken the train, it was about a twenty-minute ride. She dismissed the thought; it would take hours.

She was minutes from Mulligan's place, passing the Aigle Blanc restaurant, when she spotted Monsieur. He was sitting at an outdoor table with the same woman who had picked him up a few days back. He was three-quarters of the way turned away from her, and didn't see her, but Diana recognized the woman— her long wavy hair, the way she threw her head back to laugh. A bottle of wine was on the table between them, and the woman reached out to stroke Monsieur's hair. *Oh my god. He's cheating on her in broad daylight.*

Catching her breath, Diana hurried up the road to Mulligan's. She pressed the buzzer at Pascale's front door and waited. Expecting Pascale to open the door, she yelped when she saw Mulligan.

"Mull!" she screamed, grabbing her friend's narrow shoulders. She buried her nose in Mulligan's thick hair. It smelled like a new meadow.

"Come on in. Hey, it hasn't been that long, Di."

"Feels like ages."

"Can't wait to hear about your first two weeks." Mulligan led the way down the familiar hallway to her apartment.

Inside, Diana paused. "It looks bigger." She set her bag on the rug and swallowed hard. "Can I ask you first, before anything else, if you talked to your father?"

Mulligan sat and tucked her stockinged feet under her legs. "I did talk to him. He said that all he knows right now is that your dad is out on bail but he's under twenty-four-hour monitoring and house arrest. It was in the *Globe*. I don't know if your mom is with him in the house."

"She went to Providence with the boys," Diana said softly. "To stay with my uncle Jimmy. But if my father is back in the house…maybe she went back home, too. I don't know, I haven't heard from her."

Mulligan gnawed on her lower lip. "I wish I knew more. My dad said he read that the house and all his assets are frozen. I'm sorry, Di."

"It's weird. I should be crying, but I can't. I should be furious with him, and I am, I guess, but I feel so dead inside about this whole thing. I don't know what to feel. Sometimes, my heart lurches with the thought of it all. You know, that we might never live in the house again, that my father could end up in prison? Then I make myself stop thinking like that. Because I don't really believe it. I mean, that's not my dad. I think the feds got it wrong, but I don't know how else to explain it."

"Don't even try to explain it. You don't have enough information, and you haven't been able to talk to either your mom or your dad. Plus, you're probably still in shock," Mulligan said gently. "Plus, you're not there, so you're not in the middle of it. The news can change daily, even more frequently."

"I suppose. Not being there isn't a bad thing. I

can't even imagine my mother, and what she must be going through. Like she hasn't gone through enough already. Or Chip and Cam, trying to make sense of it, even though they're really too young to understand." Diana leaned back and stared at the ceiling. "And if I was home, I'd have to see my father under house arrest. My *father*, Mull." Her voice cracked and Diana swiped at her cheek.

"A father influences his daughter's life in so many ways. He shapes you into the woman you are, sometimes without either of you even realizing it. You measure your boyfriends against your father. I did, and no one was ever good enough. Hard to compete with the guy you think is perfect." Mulligan wouldn't look at Diana. She focused on her knees instead.

"Monsieur is cheating on Madame," Diana said, changing the subject. Mulligan jerked her head.

"What? How do you know?"

Diana explained about the woman who picked up Monsieur at the house, and seeing them together earlier. "It was too intimate to be anything other than an affair," she said, shaking her head. "What a scumbag he is. In plain sight, too."

"Wow. Do you think...?"

"What?"

"Well, I mean, if he's that brazen about it, maybe she knows? Maybe she doesn't care?"

"Mull, how can you say that? Of course she would care?"

Mulligan lowered her eyebrows. With a shrug, she replied, "Who knows, Di? Who knows about any marriage?"

Diana turned her head to look out the window, thinking about what Mulligan had said. The garden at the back of the house had one tree, covered in buds now. There was a red wooden birdhouse on a tall stick, but Diana didn't see any birds near the house. Beyond the garden and the birdhouse was an apartment building, a wall of units, four stories tall, in concrete and metal. Diana's back yard led to the rocks and the ocean, and a tiny strip of sandy beach that belonged to only them.

"Who knows," she repeated Mulligan's last words, but with a bitter edge in her voice. Her parents certainly didn't have an ideal marriage. "My father always treated me like a princess," she mused. "My mother hated that. She was probably right. I always saw her as the bad one. If she said no—to anything—I went to Daddy. I learned how to manipulate him to get what I wanted." Diana turned back to look at Mulligan. "No wonder my mother and I were always at odds with each other."

"The first man we fall in love with is dad, right?" Mulligan asked. "We compete with our mothers for the affection of one man. You represent the younger version of her, the one your father fell in love with. Then you take her place. She resents you, and you—even unknowingly—use it to your advantage."

Diana stared at Mulligan, then she nodded. Of course, she thought. No boy could ever measure up to Daddy. No one, ever, would love her as much.

FOURTEEN

Monday, June 15, 1981

Monsieur surprised Diana with news on Monday at the noontime meal. She and Madame had just set a platter of braised beef, small potatoes, and long, thin stalks of asparagus on the table. Kenny was buckled into his highchair and eyed the platter of food with suspicion.

Monsieur poured red wine for himself. Madame waved it away. He didn't offer wine to Diana, which she figured was just as well. She'd end up sleeping all afternoon if she drank wine in the middle of the day. After raising the glass to his lips and taking a long swallow, he refilled his glass and set the bottle down on the table. He turned his attention to Diana and gave her a big smile, showing his shiny Chiclet teeth and overbite.

"Diana, we will go on vacation next week. To Corsica. Do you know where Corsica is?" He lifted the glass to his lips again but kept his gaze fixed on Diana.

She hesitated. Corsica. Was he teasing her? Trying to make her look stupid? Dumb American? Corsica. Napoleon, right? It was an island in the Mediterranean Sea.

"Of course I know where it is. It's an island in the Mediterranean." *Please let me be right*, she thought.

"Good. We leave on Saturday. For one week." He grinned at his wife, who smiled shyly in return. Diana noticed that Madame was eating only a tiny bit of beef and asparagus.

Diana was incredulous. She'd been working less than a month and already they were going on vacation? She assumed she'd be taking care of Kenny the whole time, but still! No cooking or cleaning and she'd get to see Corsica. For the lousy pay, at least this job had some decent benefits.

"You will stay here in the house, how you say, keep your eye on it."

"Oh! Of course, sure. And..." She hesitated. Was she supposed to babysit Kenny for the week?

"Yes?"

"Kenny? Does he stay here with me?"

Monsieur set down his glass and gave Diana a withering look. She watched his dark eyes turn even darker and knew it wasn't a good idea to make him mad. He translated Diana's question into French for Madame, who gave Diana a questioning stare.

"Of course not. We take our son with us. We wouldn't leave him here all week." *With you.* Again he looked at Madame, said something Diana didn't understand. She watched Madame duck her head and smile.

"Sorry. *Excusez-moi.*" Diana stared down at her food and longed for a big glass of wine. She concentrated on cutting her beef into tiny pieces.

"We will leave money for you for food," Monsieur said, softer this time. "Anne," he added, and said something to his wife about money.

"*Oui, oui, demain*," she said. Tomorrow. Madame smiled at Diana, no longer laughing at her. She said something about not eating any *pâtes* until Saturday. No pasta? Oh, Diana understood. No pasta, no bread. She was trying to diet.

Money for food, plus they owed her today for the June salary that Monsieur had said would be paid to her on the fifteenth of every month. They would be gone from the twentieth to the twenty-seventh of June. So she would make sure she got everything. *Demain.* Tomorrow. Even though they were supposed to pay her today. *Aujourd'hui.*

Kenny demanded more milk. When his parents continued their conversation in French, ignoring him, he threw his plastic cup on the table, spraying Monsieur with whatever milk was left in his cup.

"*Merde!* Kenny!" Monsieur boomed. Kenny's eyes widened at the sound of his father's voice, and within seconds he was crying. Screaming. Piercing, ear-splitting screams. Diana had images in her mind of Kenny screaming in Corsica. And her, alone in the quiet Brusadin house.

She jumped up, grabbed the cup, and brought it into the kitchen. She poured milk into his bottle, filling it halfway, and secured the top. Bringing it back to Madame, she then cleared the plates and, knowing the routine, placed a small cordial glass on the table in front of Monsieur. She would remove the tablecloth when they were finished, but for the moment, it wasn't that bad.

Madame lifted Kenny from his highchair and fixed the bottle's nipple into his mouth. She cradled the boy against her chest as he sucked on the bottle.

Monsieur jerked his head at his wife, an indication to her that she should leave the table with Kenny. Could he not bear to watch his wife and son together? Was he still mad at Kenny for getting milk on him? Or was he thinking only about the dark-haired woman? And why go on vacation now when he was in the middle of an affair? Diana's earlier question about whether Kenny would go on vacation with his parents was not that outlandish, given the way they either ignored him or seemed put off by his presence. *Okay, not all the time, but really*, Diana thought—*maybe it would be better for them if they did leave him behind*. Not that she wanted to deal with Kenny for a week without his parents. But Diana wondered, did they really want this child? They were both older. Madame must have been in her mid-thirties when she got pregnant, Monsieur a little older. Was it a last-ditch attempt to have a child? Was it unplanned? She'd probably never know. She knew she would never ask.

As Madame carried Kenny into the living room and settled against the sofa cushions, Monsieur closed his eyes. Diana retrieved a bottle of cognac from the liquor cabinet and placed it on the table, next to the small glass. As Monsieur unscrewed the top of the bottle, Diana escaped to the kitchen and began washing dishes.

FIFTEEN

Diana had one hundred and fifty francs in her pocket on Saturday, when Monsieur, Madame, and little Kenny drove away from the farm to start their vacation. She had the entire house to herself! For a week!

Mulligan was going home at the end of the month, so Diana had said they should have a little party at the house. Nothing too big, she'd cautioned. "I don't want anything to happen to the house. It *cannot* get wrecked." But Mulligan could invite whichever classmates were still around. "Maybe no more than six, okay?"

"Sure, Di."

"And boys," Diana said. "Not just Renee and Pam, okay? You do know some boys, don't you?"

Mulligan laughed, and as she swept her golden hair away from her face, it caught the afternoon light and glistened, as if it held the sun in each of its strands. "Yes. You've actually been introduced to a few of them. Remember?"

"Whatever. Just invite them. And tell them to bring booze. This is probably my only chance all summer to have a summer fling."

"Is that what you want, a fling?"

"Maybe!" Diana said. "Come on, Mull. We're young and blonde and fabulous. We should have cute boys drooling at our feet. I could use something mindless."

"Ha. Okay, I'll see who's still in town. A lot of the students went home already. I think Pam might be leaving soon."

"If Renee and Pam are coming, just ask a few of them. I don't want a blowout at the house. And we have to be mostly outdoors. The Brusadins have really nice stuff."

"But you want a party. With booze. And boys."

"Yes, I do. If there are four of us, then find four boys. Or three boys. Pam has her *honey* waiting at home." Diana rolled her eyes.

❧

There was a fling, one that Diana would remember for a long time. She hadn't intended to get drunk, because she needed to be in control. The Brusadins' house was her responsibility, and anyone who had too much to drink was forced to stay outside. Charlie and Kevin, the Americans, were immature and obnoxious, and when Charlie peed into a potted geranium on the patio, Diana had had enough.

By eleven-thirty, she called it a night. Pam and Renee took their cues and herded the American boys into a car that belonged to Atsu, from Nigeria. Mulligan asked

Diana if she should stay, but Diana waved her away. "It's fine, Mull. Let Anders drive you back." Anders, the tall blond from Norway, seemed hesitant to leave, and when Mulligan went inside to use the bathroom, Anders dipped his head to Diana and whispered, "I could come back after I bring her home." His pale eyes held a promise, and Diana looked at him, considering. Her wine-fogged brain saw only a cute boy and an opportunity.

"Yes," she whispered back, waving at Atsu's car as it headed out of the driveway. "Yes, come back." A tingle of anticipation shivered down her spine. Mulligan wasn't interested in him, of that she was sure, and Anders seemed perfectly sober, and he wanted to come back! He escorted Mulligan to his Renault, held the door for her, and winked at Diana before climbing in. As he sped away, she wondered briefly if he really would return.

What if he does?! He wants to spend the night. *Why not*, she told herself. Why not enjoy the moment? She cleaned up the house, lit candles in her bedroom, and took the fastest shower she'd ever taken. There was still an unopened bottle of wine, a Chardonnay Anders had brought. She put the bottle in the refrigerator and waited. How would it be—fast and furious? Slow and languid? She wanted it all from this man she barely knew. He'd spent most of the night talking with Atsu and Renee, with whom he shared a class. Diana had hardly relaxed all evening, worried more about Charlie and Kevin and the damage they could do to the house.

Now, the tall Norwegian had promised to return, to her, for the whole night.

She checked her watch. Almost midnight. He would have dropped Mulligan off by now, she reckoned, and he should be on his way back. Unless he had to stop at his apartment first. For condoms? For something else? Or would he just decide to go home? Diana paced the small yard outside the house, then went back to her bedroom to check the candles, making sure the flames weren't anywhere close to the curtains.

The sound of tires in the gravel driveway caused her belly to lurch. She peeked out the window to see the Renault. Anders hopped from the car and Diana raced around to the front door to open it for him.

"Hi," she breathed.

"Hey," he said, taking a giant step toward her. They were just millimeters apart, standing with the door open.

"Come inside," she said, taking his hand. She closed the front door and set the lock. "I still have the wine you brought. It's in the refrigerator." She chewed her upper lip. *I'm nervous!* she thought. *He smells really good.*

"I want this to last all night," he muttered against her cheek. "All. Night. No sleeping."

Diana caught her breath. *Oh boy*, she said to herself. The wine could wait.

❧

Anders stayed until late Sunday morning, and Diana could have remained in bed with him for the entire day. Sundays were lazy days, anyway, with nearly all the merchants closed since noon on Saturday. People in town went to church in the morning and walked around the empty streets in the afternoon.

"I return to my home on the last day of June," he said softly against her ear. He left a trail of soft kisses from her ear, across her cheek, and finally on her mouth. The day outside was sunny and bright, and since Diana had neglected to pull the shade before she and Anders tumbled into bed, the light was harsh in the morning. She pulled a sheet over her skin, but his big hands found their way underneath the covering. "I'm glad we had this time."

"I wish you could stay," Diana responded, realizing she'd said the same thing to Mulligan. By the end of June, everyone she knew would be gone. Mulligan back to Boston, Renee and Pam to their hometowns, Anders back to Norway. *But you knew this, Diana. This was the so-called fling you wanted. Right?* She smiled and stroked his stubbly cheek.

"I could return tonight," he ventured, with one eyebrow raised. "When does the family return?"

"Next Saturday. I'm all alone for the entire week."

Anders grinned. "We will make these days unforgettable then, yes?" He ducked his head under the sheet.

SIXTEEN

While Madame and Monsieur were still in Corsica, the telephone rang one morning, early, before seven. Anders had left before sunrise, at half past five, and he wouldn't be back to see her until Thursday evening.

Should she answer it? Who would call so early in the day? Did a spy tell Monsieur that she'd had a party, and a sleepover guest? Were they checking up on her? She'd better pick up.

"*Bonjour. Residence Brusadin.*"

"Diana? Is that you, darling?"

She gasped at the familiar sound of his voice.

"Daddy? Oh, Daddy! I can't believe it!"

Diana dropped into a hard chair next to the telephone table. "Daddy, where are you?"

"I'm right here, in our house, sweetheart." His voice sounded like the voice of someone who had just walked away from a fire, or a car accident, those people on the television news sometimes, the people who still hadn't yet processed what had happened.

"Daddy? Are you...?" Diana faltered. What was the question? Are you guilty? Are you free? Are you a criminal? "Are you still under house arrest?"

"Now where did you hear that? From your mother?" The way he said the word 'mother,' like it was a word spiked with acid that he wanted to spit out quickly.

"No, I haven't talked to Mommy since... No. Mulligan told me. Her father read it in the *Globe*."

She heard him exhale an exasperated sigh on the other end. "Well, now you're talking to me, Diana darling. Your *father*. Not Dorothy's father, not a reporter for any of the damned newspapers, either."

"Oh, Daddy. I've been so worried about you."

"Everything is going to be just fine, dear. It was all a big misunderstanding. My lawyers are working everything out."

"Oh. Good." Diana paused, and enjoyed the feeling, as all the doubt and worry of the past few weeks dissolved. "So. Daddy, listen. It would be great to be able to use the credit card again! I've been really missing it!" She listened to silence at the other end. And counted. One. Two. Three.

"Darling, here's the thing. These bumbling idiots in the government won't lift the freeze until everything is sorted out. I'm so sorry, kitten. But you cannot use the credit card."

"Daddy, I've had to borrow money from Mulligan. I got a job, you know. Because after you got—after it happened, I didn't have any money. It's been hard here." Even as she said those last words, Diana was struck by guilt. It had been a heck of a lot harder for her father. And her mother.

"Yes, your mother mentioned your *job* when she gave me your telephone number. What in the world are you doing, Diana? You're not someone's *maid*, are you?"

"I'm a nanny. They call it an *au pair* here. I live with a family, the parents and a little boy. I live in their house with them." She wouldn't tell him how much—how little—they were paying her.

"A nanny!" A laugh burst out of him. Was he thinking of Astrid? "Oh, dear, darling Diana."

Emboldened, Diana continued. "Daddy, I was supposed to go to London, remember? For the royal wedding next month?"

"Hmmm." She could hear him shuffling papers in the background.

"Well, I don't have the money now. Daddy, could you send me a check? I'll give you the address if you don't have it. That way I can pay Mulligan what I owe her and have enough for the rest of the summer." Diana felt a formless dread in the pit of her stomach. London was fading on the map in her mind, a tiny speck being swallowed up by the English Channel.

"Oh honey. I wish I could send you everything you want. As I said, they've tied up all my funds at present."

"But—"

"Sweetheart, I need to go now. It was absolutely *wonderful* to hear your voice, my love. It did my old heart good. You enjoy your vacation."

Vacation?? Diana gripped the telephone receiver so hard she was afraid she'd break it.

"Goodbye, darling." And before Diana could utter another word, her father had hung up the telephone.

SEVENTEEN

Life resumed when Monsieur and Madame returned from their trip to Corsica. Madame looked tanned and relaxed, at least at first, but within a few days of their return, both her tan and her smile had faded.

Anders had said his goodbyes to Diana when he had visited for the final time, two days before the Brusadins returned. They had exchanged addresses, but she knew he'd never write, and with Diana's future so uncertain, she knew she wouldn't, either. Still, memories of their nights together would sustain her through the rest of the summer: his strong arms and chest, the way he trailed kisses down her neck, how he waited for her...Diana felt her face grow warm with remembrance.

Madame worked for an interior design firm, and Diana learned, through their conversations in the early morning, that design was her passion. Indeed, the Brusadins' small home was lovely, with coordinating pieces of furniture and artwork, and the right combination of colors. She knew how colors and shapes and textures all worked together, and the small home was like something from a magazine.

But Madame worked as a secretary, and Diana wondered why she hadn't been promoted to designer. Madame managed to explain that her boss, Madame Portmann, had inherited the business from her father when he died. Madame Portmann didn't have any training or education in design. Diana learned, from Madame Brusadin, that Madame Portmann would never promote her, because she was worried that Madame would be too good. Madame blushed as she said that last part, but Diana believed her. People were funny like that, and women could be really bad. Some of them were like queen bees, wanting to stand alone as the top woman in the field, aided by men and only men.

"You could leave the company," Diana said in what she knew was mangled French. "Start your own design business."

Madame shook her head sadly and lit another cigarette. It was nearly the end of June, and the evening air was moved by a light breeze. Breezes were good, as long as they pulled away the ever-present smells of the farm next door. Diana and Madame sat outside in the waning light while Kenny played quietly at Madame's feet, his stuffed rabbit as a playmate. He spoke gibberish to the toy, then bent his head to the rabbit to listen to its response. He was so intent on his conversation with the rabbit that he paid no mind to the adult discussion, nor did he shriek for attention. It was past his bedtime, but Diana wasn't about to mention it. Maybe Madame figured it didn't matter. Monsieur was out, and Diana wondered briefly if he was back with his girlfriend, if the vacation had been merely a short break from his infidelities.

"*Pas possible maintenant,*" she said, to answer Diana's question about starting her own design company. Not possible now. She continued in French to say that her husband's job was not steady and she needed to keep her position for the time being. *Ah, so her income is the more reliable income*, Diana mused silently.

Diana wondered if Monsieur and Madame ever discussed the situation, that Madame could do better. Or was it simply a foregone conclusion that Madame would remain at her dead-end job and carry Monsieur. As he went out at night, leaving his wife and child alone.

"*Il travaille ce soir?*" Is he working tonight? Diana asked.

Madame blew smoke up into the cool evening air, crushed the cigarette in a chipped red bowl, and turned to Diana. With a quick glance at Kenny, she said, "*Je suis sûre qu'il est.*" I'm sure he is.

EIGHTEEN

On the last day of June, Diana tried to prepare herself for Mulligan's departure. What a different June it had been! Not at all what Diana had imagined when she'd arrived in the middle of April. She rose early and found the coffee already percolated on the stovetop. Monsieur was still sleeping, as was Kenny, but she spied Madame outside on the patio, smoking. Pouring a cup of coffee for herself, Diana slid the door open and smiled when Madame turned around.

"*Bonjour*, Diana," she said, with her cigarette still in her mouth. Madame was seated on the low concrete slab, her legs stretched out in front of her. She was wearing bright blue slacks cropped at the ankle and a navy-and-white-striped top. Her bare toes were painted pale pink. Reluctantly, as if saying goodbye to a dear friend, she pulled the cigarette from her mouth and stubbed it into an ashtray. Diana lowered herself to the concrete next to Madame and said "*Bonjour*, Madame."

They sat in silence. Diana knew that Madame preferred to be quiet in the morning, probably due to the fact that her days were filled with chaos—whether pressures from her job or screaming from Kenny, or simply the way that Monsieur acted sometimes. This was her time, and Diana didn't want to intrude upon it.

"*Ton amie part aujourd'hui?*" Madame asked. Your friend leaves today? She remembered, Diana thought with a smile.

Diana nodded and held up two fingers. "*Deux amis.*" She didn't elaborate, and Madame didn't ask.

"*T'es triste?*"

"Yes, sad. A little, *oui, un peu,*" she said. "Um, *je vais*...to the *ville*...later, *plus tard*, to see them? To say *au revoir*?"

Madame patted Diana's arm and gave her a sad smile. "Go," she said. "Is okay."

They agreed that Monsieur would stay home with Kenny that afternoon, and Madame would drive Diana into town after the noontime meal. Madame said she would let Monsieur know, and not to worry about anything. Once Diana had said her goodbyes at the train station, she would meet them at the Plaza café at six, when Madame was through with work. Then they would have a drink, all together, and return home.

But Monsieur drank a lot at the noontime meal and was belligerent to both his wife and to Diana, saying they shouldn't have made plans without asking him. Kenny sensed the tension and cried throughout the meal, throwing himself into a tantrum before anyone could finish eating. Then Monsieur stormed out of the house on foot, yelling something in Italian from the front door before he slammed it. As Kenny continued to wail, Madame picked up the plates and headed to the kitchen.

Now what? Diana wondered. Madame would never leave her child home alone to drive Diana into town. She looked out the side window but couldn't see Monsieur anywhere on the road. *Where did he go?*

"Um, Madame? *Je peux marcher.*" I can walk. Did she realize what time it was? If Diana had to walk to the train station, she needed to leave immediately.

Madame explained, and had to say it three times for Diana to understand, that she would drive Diana to the train station so she could see her friends, but that Diana would have to keep Kenny with her. Because Madame had to return to work. And obviously, Monsieur could not be counted on for anything.

"Okay," Diana muttered. *Stupid Monsieur. What a baby.* She picked Kenny up off the floor and carried him into his room to change him. So, no nap for Kenny. "Great," Diana said aloud. "Just great."

Madame did not seem at all concerned about Monsieur; in fact, she was content to forget about him. But she did leave the front door unlocked.

Diana sat in the back with a sleepy little Kenny as Madame drove the Route de Berne. The sun was high above towering pine trees as they passed the tall apartment towers of Schönberg on the left, six stories of gray and yellow, drab concrete and sunny orange awnings, perhaps meant to offset the boring concrete. As they entered the outskirts of Fribourg, there were more and more apartment buildings on both sides, until they reached the Zähringen bridge. On the other side of the bridge, Madame drove past the cathedral, then turned uptown, on the Route des Alpes to the Rue Saint-Pierre, until she finally reached the train station.

"*Voila*, Diana," Madame said, stopping the car. She then reminded Diana to meet her (and Monsieur, Diana presumed, once he'd settled down from his own temper tantrum) at the Plaza café at six o'clock. Diana glanced at her wristwatch. Three hours with Kenny. She wondered if she could get him to nap on the grass in the park after she'd said goodbye to Mulligan and Anders.

Mulligan was standing outside the station, with two large suitcases flanking her. Her long hair was pulled into a ponytail and she wore a tan trench coat, even though it was too warm for a coat. Diana was surprised to see Pascale there, too. But where was Anders?

"Pascale! Nice to see you." Diana air-kissed her cheeks, right, left, and right again.

"When Mulligan mentioned that you were coming to say goodbye, Diana, I asked if I could join you. I hope you don't mind!" She looked down at Kenny, who stood holding Diana's hand, his mouth furiously working the ever-present binky. "And this must be Kenny!" Pascale stooped down to meet Kenny eye-to-eye. "*Salut, petit!*"

Kenny regarded Pascale with round eyes, but said nothing. *At least he's not screaming*, Diana thought.

"I wasn't expecting to have him this afternoon,"

Diana began. "Oh, it's not even worth telling you why." She rolled her eyes. "But I'm happy you're here, Pascale." Although if she was being honest, she knew her conversation with Mulligan would be different with Pascale, and Kenny, sitting there.

As if she could read Diana's thoughts, Pascale rose from her stooped position and said, "How about if I take Kenny for a little treat while you two have a moment together?"

"Really? Thank you, Pascale. I have him with me until I can meet Madame at six. I don't know if he'll go with you, though," Diana added, glancing at Kenny with apprehension.

Pascale stooped down again and whispered to Kenny in French, words that Diana was unable to follow, but they must have been magic, because Kenny let go of Diana's hand and took Pascale's. Pascale winked at Diana and Mulligan. "I have a way. We'll be back in half an hour, in time to see you off, Mulligan." She lifted a hand as she and Kenny walked away toward the park.

Diana turned to her friend. "Anders was supposed to be here, too," she said.

Mulligan smiled and shook her head. "He left word with me that he had to catch an earlier train to the airport. Didn't you two say your goodbyes already?" At the word 'goodbyes,' Mulligan made air quotes with her fingers and wiggled her eyebrows.

"Shut up. Whatever, Mull. I had my fling, and now he's heading back to Norway."

"But you liked him, didn't you?"

"Well, of course I liked him." Diana shrugged. "It was fun, but I knew it wouldn't last. At least I have the memories to get me through the rest of what I imagine will be a celibate summer."

Mulligan laughed out loud. "Come on, let's get inside while Pascale has your charge."

They found a table in the café next to the station. Diana asked for coffee.

"So, are you excited to go home?"

Mulligan blew across the top of a cup of tea. "I am, yes. I'm ready. It's all been wonderful. But I'll miss you, Diana! I'll miss Pascale, too. She's been so kind."

Diana stared into the dark depths of her coffee before dumping cream into her cup.

Mulligan watched her carefully. "Who could have predicted how things would have gone, right, Di?"

"Right," Diana muttered. She hadn't even had a chance to tell Mulligan about the phone call from her father. Diana had hoped to speak with Mulligan two days ago on Sunday, but Madame and Monsieur had offered to take Diana on a ride in the country, and Diana didn't feel that she could refuse, even though it was her day off. Of course, she was there to take care of Kenny, as she soon learned once they arrived. She dealt with Kenny while they smoked and drank and carried on a conversation she couldn't follow with other adults at the outdoor café. By the time Monsieur had decided they'd had enough, Kenny was asleep in Diana's lap. They piled back into the car and returned home.

"Diana, you're lost in thought," Mulligan remarked.

"Sorry! I'm going to miss you, too, Mull."

"Ah, you're doing just fine out there on the farm," Mulligan replied, laughing.

Diana pushed her cup away and tapped Mulligan's arm. "My father called me. I didn't want to say anything in front of Pascale."

"Oh my god. When, Di?"

"Last week. A couple of days after the party we had. He said he was calling from the house, that he got the number from my mother."

"Is everything okay?"

"No. Of course not. He said his assets are still frozen, he blames the feds, and he laughed at me when I told him I had a job."

"Oh, Diana. I'm sorry."

"The entire conversation was a waste of time," Diana said glumly. "Sorry. I shouldn't have even mentioned it. Pascale's coming back. Please don't say anything."

Mulligan leaned across to hug Diana. "Courage, my friend. I know everything will work out. And when the time comes and you're ready to fly back, just let me know. I'll take care of it, whatever you need. Don't be too proud to ask, okay?"

"You're my best friend."

"Ditto."

Pascale entered the café with Kenny, who toddled over to Diana. She lifted him onto her lap and looked up at Pascale. "Was he a good boy?"

"The best," she said, then, catching Diana's eye, she tossed her head back and laughed. "Well...he was fine. I think he could use a nap." Turning her attention to Mulligan, she said, "It's time, my dear." Pascale tucked a hand into her pocket and placed a folded ten-franc note on the table, as if it was nothing. "My treat."

NINETEEN

Monsieur told Diana that she would need to take a train to France for the day.

"*Pourquoi?* Why?"

He still gave Diana the once-over every day, but he'd never made a pass at her. Diana had no doubt that Monsieur flirted with women, and worse, and she knew Madame believed it, too. If he ever tried anything with her, she'd leave that day and go to Pascale, and Diana assumed that Monsieur knew it, which was why he behaved himself. But she couldn't stop him from his wolf-like ogling. She was careful about the way she dressed, even when the weather was hot—no shorts, no tank tops. Only when she knew he'd be out of the house.

"Because you are allowed to stay in the country—as a tourist—for three months." He held up a thumb and two fingers. "You arrived here when? April, yes?"

"April. April nineteenth."

"So. It is now the third day of July. You go to France. A town called Pontarlier. You walk around. Have lunch, then you take the train back to Fribourg. You must ask for a stamp for your passport, first time when you cross into France. Make sure you get the stamp. Tell them you collect the stamps, okay? And you must get a stamp when you return to Switzerland. *Et voila!* Another three months." Monsieur grinned, baring his big, shiny teeth.

"And it's legal?" Diana understood the Swiss were strict about the tourist visa. When she had arrived in Switzerland, she'd assumed she'd be on her way to London before the middle of July. She hadn't thought about the situation until Monsieur brought it up. They wanted her to stay through the summer, and it looked like London was never going to happen. She tried not to think too much about it, but there was no money from her father. She'd be lucky if she could watch the wedding on the Brusadins' little television set.

Monsieur's eyes traveled down her shirt, rested for a second on her breasts, and landed on her stomach. Diana sucked it in without thinking.

"Yes, Diana, it is legal."

She hesitated. How much was a train ticket to France, to this Pontarlier he mentioned? She assumed it was just over the border. Still, why should she have to pay for the ticket?

"Okay, so you will go tomorrow," he said.

Saturday was the fourth of July. How appropriate, Diana thought with a grimace. Nothing going on in Switzerland *or* France.

Monsieur turned away from her, but Diana grabbed hold of his shirtsleeve. Surprised, Monsieur raised his eyebrows. A tiny smile appeared at the corners of his mouth.

He lifted his jacket from a nearby chair and slipped into it, tugging at the lapels. Monsieur never wore a necktie, and his shirts were always unbuttoned that extra button. Is this how he dressed to sell insurance? Diana thought it was a little casual, but what did she know? If he was mainly selling to women, perhaps the look worked. *It worked on his little girlfriend*, she thought bitterly.

"You need to pay for the train ticket," she said, surprising herself by her confidence. Would he refuse? Would he counter, and say this was her problem, not his? Diana had found Madame to be far more generous than Monsieur.

But Monsieur pulled a flat wallet from the inside breast pocket of his suit jacket. He caressed the black leather with his fingertips before opening it.

He withdrew a fifty-franc note, held her gaze, then took out another. Holding the two paper bills between his fingers like a cigarette, he extended his hand to within millimeters of Diana's chest. His fingers were so close to her breast he could have grazed her with the money. She flashed back to creepy Mr. Dorrance offering her a hundred dollars to show him her bare breasts. *Pig.*

Diana swallowed down her quivery disgust, took a step back from him, and snatched the bills.

"*Merci*," she snapped, refusing to look at him.

❧

With a new stamp on her passport, Diana began the first full week of July with jaunty determination. Her language skills had definitely improved by conversing with Madame. Kenny adored her, and he even acted better during mealtime. She gently coaxed him into eating by arranging the food on his plate into shapes. It worked, most of the time, and a giggling Kenny at the table was preferable to a hysterical Kenny.

Monsieur's fortieth birthday was on the eighteenth, a Saturday, and Madame had indicated there would be an outdoor party. Of course, Diana would be working, and there was no mention of extra time off to compensate. They just assumed she had nowhere else to go. Diana realized with dull heart that they were right.

But she was resolute to be positive. *My new resolve is to take each day and find something good in it*, she told herself. *Every day offers an opportunity to learn, to improve my French, to get closer to Madame.* She wouldn't give up hope. The idea of going to London for the wedding of Charles and Diana was long gone now, and she'd had her pity-cry alone in her bedroom.

Mulligan had given Diana a present as they stood on the platform of the train station. She'd told her that she'd wanted to leave her with "words to live by," she'd said. "So I made this for you, Diana." She'd handed Diana a wrapped gift, telling her to wait and open it when she was alone. So Diana had slipped the present into her bag and carried it with her all that afternoon with Kenny, and later at the Plaza Café with Madame and Monsieur, until later that evening, when she was alone in her bedroom, she carefully removed the wrapping paper and uncovered a framed poem, that Mulligan had copied in her exquisite calligraphy. It was by someone named Sai Baba, someone Diana had never heard of. But the poem said:

Life is a song—sing it.
Life is a game—play it.
Life is a challenge—meet it.
Life is a dream—realize it.
Life is a sacrifice—offer it.
Life is love—enjoy it.

❦

Monsieur's birthday party wouldn't be a big gathering, just Madame's parents and Monsieur's friend Luigi and Luigi's wife Fiorella. Plus Madame, Monsieur, Diana, and, of course, Kenny.

Madame had typed out the menu and shopped on Friday. Besides cleaning the entire house early on Saturday morning, Diana would assist in preparation of the food.

There was Vacherin Fribourgeois and Mont Vully cheeses, and smoked ham and Swiss brioche. There was freshly ground meat from Madame's father, who ran a *boucherie* in town. In the kitchen, Madame set the ground beef in a large bowl, then added sherry vinegar, dry mustard, egg yolks (she saved the egg whites in a cup and refrigerated them). She added olive oil, shallots that

Diana helped to mince, capers. Salt and pepper and a squeeze of lemon.

"*Et voila*," she said.

"*Et maintenant quoi*?" Diana asked. Now what? How was it cooked?

"*Maintenant on le mange*," she replied. Now we eat it.

"*Mais c'est cru!*" Diana said. It's raw!

That was how Diana learned about steak tartare. It took several glasses of red wine before she could manage a small bite. *I just ate raw meat. Wait until I tell Mull.* With a pang of regret, Diana realized she'd have to write about it in a letter to Mulligan.

Madame's parents were not much interested in sitting outside, and seemed content to stay indoors. Diana wondered if maybe they preferred being inside while Monsieur was outside, regaling his friend Luigi with stories that the two of them found hilarious. Madame moved between the indoors and outdoors, but Diana thought she looked happier inside with her parents. Shortly after two o'clock, Madame stepped outside to let Monsieur know that her parents were leaving. Apparently, her father was not feeling well (Diana hoped it wasn't the raw meat). Monsieur hoisted himself from his chair in the grass to bid his in-laws goodbye. Diana carried Kenny indoors as well, leaving Luigi and his wife sitting outside.

"I hope you feel better," Monsieur said to Madame's father in French. The old man waved a hand in the air, dismissing either his own illness or Monsieur, Diana couldn't be sure. Madame's mother kissed Madame, snuggled Kenny, and offered her hand to Diana, saying something to her in French that Diana couldn't follow, but she smiled anyway and squeezed the old woman's hand. Diana noticed that neither of Madame's parents had much to say to Monsieur, and that Monsieur didn't seem to care.

A marriage that her parents didn't approve of, Diana thought. *Not unlike my parents' marriage. Grandmother didn't approve of Mommy, either—she was convinced that Daddy was marrying beneath his status. Is this how Madame's parents feel about Monsieur?*

Madame said goodbye, closed the front door, and returned to the living room. Monsieur had already gone back outside to his friends. Kenny ran to the back slider, trying to pull it open. Diana helped out, and Kenny ran across the grass to his father, who lifted him to a swing and began pushing him. The swing resembled a red plastic milk carton, and Kenny's chubby little legs poked out of the box. He squealed in delight as Monsieur pushed him. Diana stood next to Madame as she stared at her husband and child in motion. She smoked her cigarette in silence.

"*Mes parents ont toujours détesté Giancarlo.*"

Oh! Madame's parents hated Monsieur, whose name Diana learned was Giancarlo. It had taken all that time for Diana to learn his name. Giancarlo and Anne-Marie.

"*Je suis désolée,*" Diana said. Sorry that Madame's

parents had had to leave early. Sorry that they couldn't stay to balance out Monsieur's friends. Sorry that her parents couldn't stand her husband. How lonely for Madame. *I'm not sorry to avoid the drama, though,* Diana thought.

"*Eh bien,*" Madame said with a heavy sigh, "*je vais chercher le gâteau.*" I'll get the cake.

TWENTY

Luigi and Monsieur drank a lot at the party—two bottles of red wine and glass after glass of cognac from a bottle Luigi had brought. They spoke mostly in Italian, as did Luigi's wife Fiorella. Madame would say something to Monsieur, who translated it into Italian for the couple. More cheese? Some bread? Another grilled sausage? Diana tried to pick up the Italian words, but everything went so fast. She focused her attention on Kenny.

Fiorella looked to be about thirty years old, Diana guessed, maybe younger. She was olive-skinned, and her long dark hair was twisted and tied up in a knot on her head. She had a lot of dark hair on her forearms, which made them look mannish, and a trace of dark hair above her upper lip. She was heavyset, with most of her weight settled in her lower half. Her summer dress, in a bright orange flowery print, rode up in the back, and the backs of her knees were dimpled and doughy. Her legs were thick, with no definition from calf to ankle, and when she rose from her chair, she let out a tiny grunt. Diana watched Fiorella make her way back to the house, following Madame, who carried Kenny inside to lay him down for a nap. Diana remained seated, watching Monsieur and Luigi finish the bottle of cognac. She was surprised either of them was still conscious.

"*Mia moglie*," said Monsieur, seeming to notice Diana for the first time. He translated to English for her benefit, even though she wanted to tell him it wasn't necessary. "My wife," he said, drawing out each syllable as if Diana was incapable of understanding words. "*Mia moglie ha un bel corpo.*" He used his hands to make a figure eight. *Ah*, Diana said to herself. *Yes, Madame has a nice body. Where was this going?*

Luigi picked up the bottle of cognac, noticed it was empty, and tossed it on the grass, where it fell over onto its side, like a passed-out drunk.

Looking again at Diana with red-rimmed eyes, Monsieur continued. "Diana, you look good. You have a nice body, too." He swayed in his chair and stared at her chest. Diana stiffened in her chair. Why hadn't she gone inside?

"*Vecchio uomo*," Luigi slurred, laughing. His lips were thick under a black beard and mustache, and his teeth were unusually small for his mouth. He, too, turned to stare at Diana. He spoke in French, attempting to say, "She's too young for you," but he mispronounced the word *jeune* as *jaune*, in effect stating that Diana was too yellow for Monsieur. They both broke up in gales of laughter. Diana moved to leave the drunken scene, but as she was rising from her chair, Monsieur lobbed an insult at Luigi.

"*Ma tua moglie. Mio Dio.*" But your wife, my god. He spread his arms to indicate Fiorella's width. "*Obesa! Una balena!*"

Balena? What is that? Not anything good, Diana reasoned. The mood was darkening between the men; after all, Monsieur had just insulted Luigi's wife.

Diana was glad neither Madame nor Fiorella was present, especially Fiorella, who was just called *una balena*, and she excused herself to retreat indoors. She found the two women seated at the dining room table, drinking coffee.

"Diana. *Assis-toi*. Please." Madame indicated a chair next to her, then poured coffee into a small cup and slid it across the table. Diana took a sip of the hot and bitter liquid, but did not ask for sugar. The bitterness was appropriate after that exchange between the men. She glanced outside at Monsieur and Luigi, who looked to be arguing with each other, but they were both so crocked, Diana doubted either of them could have stood up.

The women sat in silence, while Kenny slept in his room down the hallway. Diana glanced outside again and the two men seemed to be sleeping, too.

When Luigi and Monsieur stumbled into the house forty minutes later, Fiorella hoisted herself from her chair and spoke sharply to her husband in Italian.

"*Nous partons*," she said to Madame. Monsieur dropped to the couch and closed his eyes. Diana wished she had one of those silly conical birthday hats. She'd slip it on him and take a picture. The forty-year-old on his birthday.

Fiorella kissed Madame and shook Diana's hand. With a withering look at her husband, she held out her hand, palm up, and waited, until Luigi dug into his pocket and placed the car keys in her hand. Luigi mumbled his thanks and goodbye to Madame, peeked shyly at Diana, and followed his wife out the door.

∂✿

The following Wednesday brought excessive heat and humidity. All summer up until that day, the weather had been comfortably warm, sometimes rainy, but humidity was a rarity. Once Madame and Monsieur had left for work, Diana changed back into shorts and a tank top. Kenny had woken and eaten, and Diana had played with him for an hour, but by ten-thirty in the morning he was ready for another nap. Diana had learned that by engaging him in plenty of outside play before Madame and Monsieur arrived back home at noon, he'd be better behaved at the table and easier to put down in the afternoon. And having him asleep in his room while she cleaned was preferable. Kenny still had the occasional tantrum, desperate for attention from his parents, but he listened to Diana when it was just the two of them. She read books to him, sang to him. There was a song that Madame sang, and had taught to Diana, that she would sing to Kenny.

It was a simple song that Kenny loved. Even Diana

understood the lyrics. You need someone who will take your hand, a little like a guardian angel. Just someone you know well. Don't go looking too far. The song became almost a lullaby for Kenny, and Diana hummed it to herself as she worked.

In the oppressive heat, Diana felt trickles of sweat run down her back. The cotton tank top was plastered against her body. She drank a bottle of water and tried to fan her face with a magazine, but the little house was airless. She'd finish her work, take a cooling shower, and change back into long pants and a shirt before Madame and Monsieur arrived home for lunch.

She turned on the radio, not too loud, and sang along with "Bette Davis Eyes." *What a strange song*, she thought. Still, it was American music.

As she moved out of the kitchen and into the living room, she gasped. Luigi had let himself in through the unlocked sliding door at the back of the house. He stood, massive, in the living room, staring at her.

"Hey! You can't just walk in here," she cried, folding her arms over her chest, aware of her exposure. She knew he wouldn't understand English, but the tone of her voice was unmistakable. "Get out, please. *Il faut partir, maintenant, monsieur.*"

"*Mais non,*" he crooned, and in two long steps he was within inches of her. "*Sembri deliziosa.*" Diana tensed. What was she going to do? He was a big man. If she screamed, no one would hear her. Only Kenny. The drone of a tractor was way off in the distance.

He laid a hairy paw on her bare shoulder, and Diana instinctively stepped back. He stepped forward, gripped her shoulders with both hands, and walked her back into the kitchen, where he pressed her against the kitchen counter. "No," Diana said, as he slipped his fat fingers beneath the strap of her top. Diana wished desperately that she'd kept her bra on. He leaned on her, his hot breath in her face, his full weight pinning her down.

"Stop," Diana croaked, her voice not strong enough. But now Luigi was pushing his stomach against her, hard. The rim of the counter dug into the small of her back. His giant hands were on her, and one pulled the strap of her tank top off her shoulder. The other tugged at her elastic-waisted shorts. Each time Diana tried to move he pushed harder. His massive bulk rendered her immobile. His knee dug into her thigh, and her back hurt from the pressure on the sharp edge of the counter. He pressed his face into her neck. Scratchy and rough, like the coarsest sandpaper. He would ravage her skin. He shoved his hand inside her shorts, inside her underwear, and muttered in Italian. Gutteral, animal noises as his fingers violated her. She felt his hardness against her and her mind raced. *I cannot let this happen. No no no.* Her hands scrabbled behind her on the counter.

"No, please," she cried. Where was her strength? "Please. Stop."

His fingers were farther inside her, moving. She couldn't escape his fingers. Salty tears ran down her face, landing on her lips. His sweaty face against hers. The smell of him, she wanted to vomit. She felt his teeth, those small teeth, on her neck. She burned with shame, helpless against the pig that was going to rape her. She knew he would. He would do it standing up if he had to, but she knew that was his aim. She fumbled behind her, her own fingers feeling their way along the counter until she had grasped the wooden handle of a utensil.

In one swift motion, she arced her arm and with all her might she plunged the fork into his arm. It didn't go deep, but Luigi screamed and pulled back. Three drops of blood appeared immediately on his arm. *Good*, Diana thought.

Wild, Diana waved the fork, wishing it was a knife instead. It didn't matter, she would poke him full of holes if she had to. "Get out!" she screamed. "Get out!"

Red-faced and sweaty, Luigi covered his forearm with his other hand and fled from the house as Kenny started to cry.

TWENTY-ONE

The wedding of Prince Charles and Lady Diana Spencer took place on a Wednesday at the end of July.

Diana had turned the television on before Madame and Monsieur arrived home. Madame had wisely prepared the noontime meal in advance, and Diana had put the dish in the oven ahead of time. They ate quickly and moved to chairs in front of the television, to see the future princess arrive in a glass coach pulled by white horses. Kenny sat contentedly on Madame's lap, sucking on his binky and twirling his dark curls around his fingers, but he showed no interest in the wedding.

Of course Monsieur had something critical to say about it. He poured himself a small glass of Galliano and smirked at the television. "It's just another day, Anne," he complained. "It's not like *you're* the bride." Then he turned to look at Diana. "What about you? You have her name," he said, pointing to the television screen, where a resplendent Diana was emerging from her Cinderella carriage. "When will you meet your prince?"

"Ssh," Anne admonished.

It had been a week since the assault, and Diana hadn't said a word to either of them. Nothing about Luigi, nothing about his intrusion into their home, about what he did to her. She kept it all inside, and only allowed herself to cry at night, alone in her bedroom, where great heaving sobs wracked her body. She would never tell Monsieur about it, because she knew he wouldn't believe her. And Madame? Diana couldn't find the words to tell her. She decided it was easier to just forget about it. Only she couldn't, she relived the moment every day. Oh, if only Mulligan was still around.

Madame had noticed a change in Diana though, asking her if she felt ill. Diana ate little at noontime, and stayed quiet in the presence of Madame and Monsieur. With her friends gone, she remained with the Brusadins throughout the weekends, even though she was technically off work. *It doesn't matter*, she told herself. *Probably best to keep busy*. She turned her attention to the television.

Charles and Diana stood at the altar in St. Paul's Cathedral. The bride looked petrified. *Well, that's understandable*, Diana thought. As she sat in the living room of the little white house on the edge of the farm, she watched the throngs of people who had gathered in London to cheer on the fancy carriage and its cavalry. Such heraldry! When she tried to imagine herself there, maybe even in the cathedral as a guest, a sadness within her deepened. If only her father hadn't been arrested. If she had been able to travel to London, she wouldn't have taken the job. She wouldn't have moved in with the Brusadins. And she wouldn't have been violated by Luigi. Diana swiped at her cheeks as tears of regret spilled from her eyes.

"Oh, you're crying," Monsieur teased. "Everyone cries at weddings. Women cry because they cannot help themselves. Men cry because they realize they've just made the biggest mistake of their lives!" Monsieur laughed at his joke. Diana ignored him.

"Do you like her dress?" Madame asked softly. Diana knew she was trying to diffuse Monsieur's snub.

"It's very...big," Diana said, because she didn't know the French word for puffy. "But she is beautiful."

"Too much dress," Monsieur pronounced. "Too many clothes." He leered at Diana.

"It's a wedding gown," Diana snapped. "It's appropriate. I suppose you would prefer she wear lingerie."

"At least the prince could see what he is getting," Monsieur scoffed. "I don't believe she is still a virgin."

"You're an idiot," Diana said before she could take it back. She saw Monsieur rear back in shock, his face hardening, and before she could say anything worse, she ran out of the room.

Madame called her name, but Diana ignored them both. She sat on the closed toilet seat in the small bathroom, the room with just a toilet and sink, what the Swiss referred to as the "WC," for water closet. They called it a powder room at home, Diana had told them, remembering the small room off the kitchen in their

Newport house, the one her mother had decorated with seashells. From her vantage point on the commode, she looked directly at the closed door. Pinned to the inside door was a poster of Julio Iglesias, Madame's favorite singer. He grinned at Diana, with perfect white teeth and a slight overbite. He wore an open-collar white shirt. Above his name on the poster, it said "*Aimer la vie.*" Love life.

It must have been an album cover. Diana stared at Julio Iglesias for what seemed like a long time, until she heard a soft tapping on the door.

"*Diana, ça va? Il faut partir.*" Are you okay? We have to leave.

Diana opened the door and cocked her head to indicate the poster on the back side. "Julio Iglesias," she said.

"*Oui, Julio. Mon prince!*" She extended her hand to Diana.

"If only," Diana replied.

❧

A few evenings later, as July slipped into August, the family drove into the town of Fribourg to watch the fireworks display for Swiss National Day.

Everyone, it seemed, had come into town.

Monsieur found a parking spot for his little car near the Plaza café. Diana held Kenny's hand tightly, remembering the day he'd run into the street, before she even knew who these people were. Most of the tables at the café were occupied, but Monsieur snagged one at the back, along the edge of a side street. He seemed upset that he couldn't get one of the tables in front, where presumably the fireworks viewing would be better. Diana would be just as happy to walk over to the Route des Alpes when the fireworks started. She stooped to Kenny's level and whispered to him that he must stay with them, did he understand? Kenny looked at Diana with his big round eyes and nodded.

"You're my responsibility," she continued, even though Kenny couldn't understand. She leaned in to whisper in his ear. "I care about you more than they do."

Monsieur raised his hand for a waiter and ordered three beers.

"No," Diana said, and turned her face up to the waiter. "*Henniez*," she said, opting for bubbly water instead.

"It's a holiday, Diana. You should celebrate." His eyes challenged her.

"It's not *my* holiday, Monsieur, and I *am* celebrating. With Henniez."

When the drinks arrived, Monsieur asked for apple juice for Kenny, and a plate of *ramequins au fromage*, little cheese pies. "Will you eat?"

"Yes. *Merci*." She turned to Madame and asked about the fireworks. It would be at least another hour before the show, Madame explained, and, as Diana had anticipated, they would walk to the Route des Alpes for better viewing.

Monsieur took a long drink from his *canette* and

looked around at the crowd. Suddenly he stood, raised his arm. "Luigi! *Ici!*"

Diana froze. There he was. Luigi plodded toward the table, squeezing his bulk between the crowded tables. Diana was trapped in her chair, unable to move. She wanted to run, to fly, to melt into the ground. She could feel it all over again, the pressure of his knee, his scratchy face, his hot, rancid breath, his fingers. Like an ugly echo, it reverberated within her, and she began to shake uncontrollably. She sat on her hands and pressed her knees together under the table.

"*Salut, Luigi,*" Madame said, turning her face up to let him kiss her cheeks. "*Ou est Fiorella?*" She looked around for Luigi's wife.

In Italian, he spoke to Monsieur, who translated for Madame. "She's sick. Pregnant." Diana sat silently and watched him. He averted making eye contact with her and he kept his left hand behind his back.

At the news of Fiorella's pregnancy, Monsieur hooted and clapped Luigi on the shoulder. He said something to him in Italian and they both snorted with laughter. When Luigi brought his hand around to scratch his head, Monsieur paused. Madame saw the bandage and asked, "*Qu'est-ce que c'est que ça?*" What's this?

The waiter set a plate of eight bite-sized *ramequins au fromage* on the table as Monsieur grabbed an extra chair from a nearby spot and set it between himself and Madame. Diana tugged on the waiter's sleeve and pulled him down so she could whisper to him. He looked at her for a moment, then nodded and hurried away.

I am not weak, Diana told herself. *He will not win.* She stared at Luigi until he finally glanced her way. She set her jaw and gave him the hardest, meanest look she could muster, even as her legs trembled beneath the table. *I did nothing wrong. He is a monster. I'm glad I stabbed him and I would gladly do it again.*

As Luigi stumbled through a lie about his injured arm, mangling the French words, the waiter returned and set a fork on the table, to the left of Diana's plate. The *ramequins au fromage* were small cheese quiches, and Madame and Monsieur had simply lifted them and taken their bites. Diana held the fork in her hand and continued to stare at Luigi.

"*Pourquoi une fourchette*, Diana?" Madame asked, laughing. "*Ce n'est pas nécessaire.*" She lifted her *ramequin* again to demonstrate.

"Ah, the Princess Diana," Monsieur taunted.

Diana turned her attention to Monsieur. "This fork? This fork saved my life," she stated. Monsieur gave her a peculiar look and laughed derisively. He picked up his *canette* as Diana twirled the fork in her hand, staring at Luigi.

Luigi coughed and pushed back in his chair. When the waiter asked him what he wanted, he replied, in his mangled French (*I speak French a lot better than he does*, Diana said to herself), that he had to leave.

"Why are you leaving?" Monsieur asked. "Stay! The fireworks will start soon."

"*Non, non,*" he mumbled, hoisting himself from the

chair. He glanced again at Diana, who stared back hard and held her fork tightly.

"Bye bye," she sang out. Madame gave her a sharp, disapproving look, but Diana ignored her. Kenny, who sat on Madame's lap, opened his eyes and echoed Diana. "Bye bye!" he chirped.

Monsieur stood up as well, first glaring at Diana, then telling his wife that he was going to take a walk with Luigi.

Once they were gone, Madame admonished Diana for her rudeness.

"*Pourquoi étais-tu si grossier?*" Madame asked.

"*Grossier?*" Gross? Rude? Whatever, Diana knew what she was asking. But how to explain? Could she find the words?

Diana craned her neck to see Monsieur and Luigi down the street, standing in front of a closed boutique. Monsieur lit a cigarette. She turned toward Madame. Kenny had fallen asleep.

"Luigi...*il est un cochon.*" He's a pig. Faltering, she attempted to tell Madame that he had come to the house after Monsieur's birthday party, that he walked in without knocking, and that he touched her. As she failed with the French words, her body began to shake violently. She worked to steady her voice, keeping her eyes on little Kenny. She couldn't find the right terms to describe the hell he had put her through, so she kept repeating "*il est un cochon.*"

Madame sat very still, then reached her free arm out

to put it around Diana's shoulders. "*C'est affreux, vraiment affreux,*" she said. Diana didn't know what she was saying, but her arm was comforting. "*Il rentre en Italie.*" He is returning to Italy.

"*Quand?*" When? How soon?

"*La semaine prochaine, je pense.*" Next week, I think.

Diana exhaled loudly. She picked up Madame's half-full *canette* and finished the beer in it. Turning to Madame with a sad smile, she said, "*Affreux.*"

"*Oui,*" Madame replied.

TWENTY-TWO

Diana had Sundays off, but with Mulligan and the rest of the Americans long gone, she didn't really have anyone to hang out with. Nothing exciting happened in Düdingen, or Fribourg for that matter. That changed when Pascale called and invited Diana to a party.

"It's this coming Saturday, Diana, and you're welcome to stay overnight in Mulligan's old room. I have promised it to a new American student, but whoever it is won't be arriving until early September. I've invited a few business colleagues and friends, and don't worry, everyone speaks English!" She chuckled on the other end of the line.

"You'd be surprised at me, Pascale. My French has improved a lot."

"I believe it. Please say you'll come. It isn't fancy."

"Yes, of course I'll come. Thank you for asking me."

"I'll come by and pick you up around four next Saturday."

Pascale had said it wasn't fancy, but Diana knew Pascale would look impeccable. Diana had only brought one summery dress, because she had expected to buy a wardrobe of new clothes in London. Maybe Madame would be willing to lend her something.

She focused on scrubbing the bathtub while Kenny slept. When she entered Monsieur and Madame's bedroom to make the bed, she noticed a stain on the bedsheet. Diana couldn't remember ever finding an indication that Madame and Monsieur had had sex, and she was surprised she hadn't heard them. Quiet sex. As she stripped off the sheets, she paused, remembering. And for the third time that morning, she checked the locks on the front door and the sliding glass door at the back of the house. But Luigi and Fiorella were definitely gone. Madame had whispered the news to her the previous day. Monsieur and Luigi had gone out on Saturday night, without their wives, and Madame had told Diana that she was just as happy.

"*Aujourd'hui ils partent*," she had said to Diana on Sunday morning. They were in the kitchen, just feet away from Monsieur at the dining room table. *Today they leave.* Diana was buoyed by the news.

After she made the bed, she checked on Kenny. He was cooing nonsense to his stuffed rabbit and didn't notice her. She'd have a few more minutes of quiet before getting him up.

A party at Pascale's! An evening where she could speak English! With smart people! Diana allowed herself to feel excited about the prospect of intermingling with interesting people. *Of course Pascale's friends would be interesting*, she thought.

The doorbell rang and Diana jumped. No one ever came to the house. The thought of Luigi darkened her thoughts for an instant. *No, he's gone. Madame said so.* Besides, why would Luigi ever ring the doorbell?

Maybe it was the Swiss-German farmer from next door. Diana saw him rarely, and when she did, she raised her hand in greeting, but they had never spoken. His name was Hans, and once, in the early days of her employment, Diana was tasked with buying a dozen eggs from the farm. She had walked across the gravel driveway to the farmhouse and knocked. When the door opened, she stared into the face of the farmer Hans—he had thin white hair on the top of a tanned skull, and his face was brown and leathery, but he smiled at her kindly. His piercing blue eyes softened as she struggled to speak German.

"*Guten Morgen,*" she said. She couldn't speak German to save her life, but she needed a dozen eggs. Diana knew the word for egg—*Ei*—from signs around Switzerland, where every product was listed in German, French, and Italian, and she could count to ten in German, thanks to a governess who had taught her when she was six (*funny the things you remember*, she thought). She smiled back at the farmer and said, "*Ei, bitte.*" And using her fingers to count to herself, she said, "*Zehn und....zwei.*" Ten and two.

The farmer had grinned at her, displaying a mouth of missing teeth, but had disappeared into the house and returned with a basket of twelve fresh eggs. Diana paid him with the money Madame had given to her and thanked him. "*Danke.*"

The doorbell rang again, jolting Diana back to the present. Taking one of the sharp knives from a drawer in the kitchen, she held it in her right hand while she opened the door with her left. The knife hung by her side, ready.

On the other side of the door was a smartly-dressed woman, about fifty years old, Diana guessed. She peered at Diana behind oversized, tortoise-shell glasses, as if she had come to the house to conduct an inspection. Diana loosened her grip on the knife.

"*Bonjour,*" Diana said, smiling. Avon lady? Do they have them in Switzerland?

"Good morning," the woman responded in accentless English. She clasped the handle of a purse with both hands and stood very straight and tall. Regal, almost, like Queen Elizabeth.

"Oh! You speak English! Hello." Diana took a step back and opened the door wider.

"Yes, most of us do speak English, you know." Her tone was brusque and businesslike, and her comment made Diana wonder if Madame maybe really knew more English than she let on. She'd have to test it out when Madame came home.

"Um...the Brusadins are not at home," Diana said. She wasn't afraid of the woman, but she was obviously there on some kind of serious matter. Diana set the knife on a table behind the half-open door.

"But it's *you* I came to see!" The woman narrowed her eyes at Diana. "You are Diana, the *au pair*." It was a statement, not a question. The woman smiled, showing her teeth. The bottom row was crooked. There was a bit of lipstick on one front tooth.

Diana had a strange rolling in her gut, a queasiness, as if from eating something spoiled. Something was about to happen, something she couldn't control. She cut her eyes to the knife on the table, hidden from the stranger's view.

"I am Madame Portmann, of Portmann Design. Where Madame Brusadin works."

"Oh! Did something happen to Madame? Is she okay?" As if the temperature had suddenly plummeted, Diana felt a chill pass over her body. *Please let Madame be all right.*

"She is fine." *Whew.* Diana held her hand over her chest. The woman stood ramrod straight in front of her, showing no emotion.

Is Madame Portmann going to offer me a job? Perhaps Madame had told her that I was good with Kenny, was good at cleaning the house. "Would you like to come inside, Madame?" Diana opened the door wider and hoped Madame Portmann wouldn't notice a knife sitting on the entrance table.

"No, thank you. Tell me, Diana, when did you arrive in Switzerland?" Steely-gray eyes bored into Diana. She hesitated. She had arrived in April, but then Monsieur made her take that trip to Pontarlier in France so she could get a new stamp on her passport. She blinked at Madame Portmann, her mouth unable to work. *Why was she asking? I got a new stamp on my passport, just like Monsieur had instructed me to do.*

"I see. Your silence is an answer to my question." Madame Portmann leaned in closer to Diana and lowered her voice, even though there was no one around. Diana could see the creases around her eyes, the tiny broken blood vessels on her nose, a mole on her cheek, with two hairs sprouting out of it.

"You will finish this little job of yours at the end of the month. Then you will return to America," she said, spitting out the word 'America.' "You have spent all the time in Switzerland that you are permitted. Do we understand each other, Diana?"

"Yes," Diana whispered. Her father had been arrested. If Diana didn't do what Madame Portmann said, she could be arrested, too. Was she in the country illegally *now*? She didn't trust Monsieur to do the right thing, but surely Madame wouldn't let something bad happen to her, right? *Right??*

"Wonderful!" Madame Portmann crowed. Her pinched mouth turned upwards. "So very nice to make your acquaintance, Diana. Have a good trip back to America." She patted her helmet hair and disappeared down the walkway.

Diana closed the front door softly, turning the bolt to lock it. She walked, robot-like, to Kenny's room, where the little boy lay awake, quiet, as if he knew something was wrong. She lifted him from his crib and held him tightly against her.

"Come on, big boy. Need a change? Okay, let's do it." She continued talking to him through his diaper change, then she lowered him to the floor. He found her hand.

"Eye-ah," he said, the best he could manage with her name. Her fingers closed around his plump little hand and she blinked furiously.

Diana brought Kenny outside into the warm August sun. They sat together on a wooden glider under a shady tree, Kenny curled into Diana's arm. Diana began singing the song about finding someone, someone like a guardian angel.

TWENTY-THREE

Diana wrote a letter to Mulligan that afternoon, once the noontime meal was eaten, Madame and Monsieur had returned to work, and Kenny had gone down for his nap. In her letter she told Mulligan everything—the visit from Madame Portmann, Pascale's upcoming party, and finally, she wrote about the sexual assault. Finding the words was so hard—how to write about something so horrific, so terrifying? Time and time again Diana had gone back in her mind. *If only.* If only I had locked all the doors. If only I hadn't been wearing such skimpy clothes. If only I'd fought harder. She emphasized to Mulligan that she was okay. Her attempts at telling Madame had, she believed, fallen flat, probably due to the language. Saying that Luigi "touched" her didn't even begin to explain what he had done to her. Writing it out to Mulligan brought some catharsis, at least. 'And please, Mull,' she wrote, 'if you write or talk to Pascale, please don't mention it. I just want to forget it ever happened.'

She ended the letter by letting Mulligan know she'd by flying home at the end of August. 'I'm going to ask

Pascale to help me find a cheap, one-way flight,' she wrote. 'I have two hundred francs, Mull. I don't know if that will be enough. I'm so sorry to have to ask, but I might need to borrow a little more. You know I'll pay you back as soon as I can. I guess this adventure wasn't quite what I had expected it to be.' Diana reread that last line and actually laughed out loud. "'Wasn't quite what I had expected it to be'? That's the understatement of 1981," she said to no one but herself.

Diana reread the lines she'd written in her neat cursive. She thought she'd live in Switzerland for a few months, easily picking up the tab for dinners and drinks with Mulligan, living her charmed life. She thought she'd fly over to London, meet influential people via her father. She thought she'd witness Lady Diana Spencer marry Prince Charles, not just watch it on a small television in a small house. She thought she might even meet her own prince. Diana laughed bitterly. *Just goes to show me*, she thought, *that John Lennon was right*. Life is what happens while you're busy making other plans.

She squeezed in a few more words at the bottom of the onion skin paper. 'I miss you, Mull. Hope everything is good. See you soon.'

Once she had addressed the letter to Mulligan, she took another paper-thin sheet of air mail stationary and began to write a letter to her parents. In it, she was upbeat and bland. The weather, the food, Kenny. She sent her love to Chip and Cam, and let her parents know that she'd be home soon. She signed off with 'love,

Diana' and folded the letter to fit in its thin envelope. What more could she say? She still didn't know what would happen to her father, but as the days passed, she believed more and more that the outcome could be bad for him.

☙

Diana didn't tell Madame about the visit from Madame Portmann. Why? If Madame Portmann had told Madame, then Madame already knew, and would make *sure* that Diana understood she had to leave the country by the end of the month. And if Madame *didn't* know, then telling her would serve no purpose, either. It would be upsetting to Madame to know that her boss had taken it upon herself to visit Madame's home and speak directly to Diana. The indisputable fact was that Diana had to leave the country by the end of August.

Even as she addressed the envelope to her mother, she knew she needed to speak with her, or with her father. But she couldn't pay for an international call, and the main telephone/telegraph center in Fribourg was closed on Sundays, her only day off.

☙

Later that evening, explaining that she needed to call home, Diana was grateful when Madame allowed her to use the home telephone.

"*Pas trop longue?*"

"No, not too long," Diana said. She would call the house in Newport. If her father was still on house arrest, he'd be there. Her mother hadn't written in weeks. Diana worried about her, and about her younger brothers. How were they coping? It was a lot to handle, and the boys weren't even teenagers yet. How would they view their father? Win Driscoll spent a lot of time in his office, and little time playing with his sons. He was older, not unlike Monsieur, who was similarly detached from Kenny. With their mother in and out of depression, she wasn't a steady presence in the boys' lives, either. And while their father provided economic support and a comfortable lifestyle, something Chip and Cam weren't even aware of, his role was to be one of the two sources of their well-being. Diana thought back to her own childhood—raised more by her governess and the cook than her mother or father. Back then, her mother reveled in her wealthy lifestyle, her social status, things she hadn't known at all in her youth. Win and Evelyn Driscoll were patrons of the arts, attending everything from the Newport Jazz Festival to the opening of the Newport Rugby Club. After the boys were born, Diana noticed her mother withdraw more and more, and her father stayed away from home more and more. All the possessions couldn't buy her peace of mind, couldn't fill her with joy.

Madame arranged that Diana would call home the following evening, when Monsieur was out. Diana figured that Madame hadn't told Monsieur about the long-distance call, or its subsequent charges. She'd noticed that Madame seemed to pay the bills. If the cost of the call had to come out of her meager allowance, so be it.

※

On Tuesday evening at six o'clock, Diana pressed buttons, first for the country code, then her full telephone number, including area code, and she waited nervously for the connection to go through.

Finally, there was a voice on the other end, but it wasn't her father's baritone that greeted her.

"Mom? Is that you?"

"Diana." Her mother's voice was flat and hollow. Diana tried to picture her, her face sagging with cheerlessness, her shoulders drooped with the weight of sadness.

"Mom! You're home!" That had to be good news, right? *Right??*

"This is no longer home, Diana." She exhaled a loud sigh on the other end of the phone, four-thousand miles away. "Your father is going to plead guilty to the charges. We're losing the house. We're losing everything." Her tone was monotonous. Her words hung in the air, like the dark clouds that had gathered outside.

Diana drew in her breath so sharply she felt a pain in her chest. "Guilty? So he did it? He stole from his clients?" How could he have done that? Why?

"Yes. He will plead guilty to three felonies. Your father is going to a federal prison, Diana. He has shamed us forever. Our name is worth nothing, it is dirt."

Diana steadied her breathing, aware of Madame sitting in the next room. "But Mom, why are you ho—why are you in the house?"

"I'm allowed to take clothes for myself and the boys. And for you, if you want. Just what we need. Your brothers are still with your Uncle Jimmy in Providence. We'll all be living there for the foreseeable future." Diana heard another long sigh on the other end. She desperately wanted to embrace her mother, to tell her that everything would be all right, but she could do neither. And would everything be all right? Diana was doubtful.

"Are the boys okay, Mommy?"

"We're all doing the best we can, dear. When are you coming home?"

Diana paused. She couldn't possibly ask for money, not now. "Um, at the end of the month. I'm just trying to make sure I have enough money to fly home."

"Yes. Well, I hope it's been a fun vacation for you."

"It wasn't a vacation, Mom! I've been working all summer. I just haven't made much money!"

"Diana, you've always had a problem understanding the value of money. You've always enjoyed spending on yourself." Diana could hear her mother shuffling items and imagined her packing boxes. "There isn't any *money*, dear. Your uncle helped me to find a two-bedroom apartment in Silver Lake, not far from him. It's owned by a friend, and he's given me a break on the rent. It should be manageable. But there isn't any extra room. If you need to stay on the couch when you get home, of course that's fine. Life will be very different from now on, Diana. You might as well get used to that now."

"Mom, I have to go. This call is too expensive."

"Yes, I'm sure it is. Thank you for not calling collect. I'll send you our new address and phone number. Come home and get on with your life, Diana. It's all any of us can do. Goodbye."

The line went dead, and Diana set the receiver back in its cradle as softly as she could. She took a step into the living room and met Madame's eyes. Without speaking, she knew Madame recognized Diana's emotions. *I will not cry*, she vowed silently.

"*Ça va*, Diana?"

Diana nodded. Chewing her bottom lip, she slumped into a chair next to Madame. But she couldn't speak. She didn't trust her voice. *I would stay here if I could*, she thought. *But I can't*.

Madame tilted her head toward Diana, then reached out to stroke her hair. That one gesture, so motherly, so caring, undid Diana, and she dissolved into tears.

"I know you can't understand me, Madame, but I can't speak French tonight. I can't speak well enough for you to understand me! All summer long I've tried to do my best, and I have nothing to show for it. My father is a criminal and he's going to jail. That's what my mother just told me on the telephone. Out house is no longer our house, and it was a really nice house, Madame. But it was all a lie. A house of sand, nothing. My life, my enchanted life, it was all a lie." She gulped air into her lungs, oblivious to Madame. She continued her soliloquy.

"I have to go home soon. Your boss showed up here and basically demanded it. Monsieur fixed it so that I had enough time on my passport, but she knows I've been here longer than three months, and if I don't leave by the end of the month, she'll probably call the authorities on me and I'll end up in jail just like my father. So I fly home with nothing, to nothing. I don't even know what to do next." She stared hard at her hands. She and Madame had painted their fingernails over the weekend and the pink polish looked pretty. Finally she turned her wet eyes to Madame. "Sorry. I've been ranting in English and you don't even understand."

"Diana," Madame crooned, as if she was speaking to a drowsy Kenny. "*Tout finira bien.*" Everything will be okay in the end. She gave Diana a sad smile. Then she stood up and disappeared into the kitchen. When she came back, she was carrying an open bottle of red wine. "*Buvons!*" she said happily. Let's drink.

Why not, Diana reasoned. Why not, indeed.

TWENTY-FOUR

Diana borrowed a dress from Madame for Pascale's party. It was sleeveless and yellow and perhaps not the best color for her complexion, but she liked the way she looked in the dress, with its low back and flouncy hem. Madame put mousse in her hair and made up her eyes, too heavy with eyeliner, Diana thought. But it was a different look, maybe more sophisticated.

"Tu vas peut-être rencontrer un homme sympa?" Madame asked softly. Diana closed her eyes as Madame enveloped her head with hairspray.

Maybe I will *meet a nice guy*, Diana thought. *"Peut-être,"* she replied. Although it wouldn't really matter, since she was flying home in a couple of weeks. She'd had her summer fling with Anders, and there had been no communication from him. She hadn't written, either, preferring to keep the memory of their time together a memory.

"Ça va bien, Diana? Oh-kay?"

Diana nodded. She swallowed down a lump in her throat, one that had threatened too frequently in the past week.

"*Triste de partir.*" Sad to leave. Madame raised her eyebrows.

Diana pressed her tongue to the roof of her mouth. "*Oui,* Madame."

"*Amuse-toi bien! Embrasse un étranger!*" Have fun! Kiss a stranger!

❧

Pascale arrived promptly at four o'clock, and Diana hurried outside to meet her. For reasons she couldn't explain, Diana did not want Pascale and Madame to meet. She carried Madame's high heels in one hand, her smaller suitcase in the other for the overnight stay. She made sure to pack a sleep shirt and comfortable clothes for the next day, and she wore her sandals, knowing the high-heeled shoes would hurt.

Pascale was standing outside her car. "I would have come to the door, Diana. You didn't have to rush out. We've got plenty of time."

"It's fine. We can go now."

"Ah," Pascale said slowly. "Okay, Diana. Your worlds will not collide." She used her hands to indicate two planets encircling each other, then chuckled and slid into the driver's seat. She shifted the car into reverse, backed up the gravel driveway, and turned out onto the road.

Pascale drove more deliberately than Monsieur, and Diana had a chance to view the surroundings as they drove to Fribourg. Pascale took a different route than the one Diana normally walked when she and Kenny strolled into town in the afternoons. It was more circuitous, but as Pascale had said, they had plenty of time.

"You look pretty," she remarked, without taking her eyes off the twisty road ahead.

"Thanks," Diana replied, ducking her head. "I know you said it wasn't fancy, but I wanted to look nice. Madame did my makeup. Is it too much?"

Pascale grinned. "Not at all! And yellow is a good color on you."

Diana smiled at the compliment. The scenery outside the town was all the same: vast expanses of farmland dotted with barns and houses. "I've been here for months, and I don't think I've ever come this way," she said. "When I walk into town with Kenny, we always follow the Route de Berne."

"I just thought it would be nice for you to see something different," Pascale said.

"It is," Diana said, as Pascale maneuvered the car over the old bridge. Below, the Sarine River glistened under the afternoon sun. Pascale pointed out the Baroque-style building of the Loreto Chapel, the Montorge Monastery, and the public swimming pool.

"Oh! That pool looks wonderful. I'm sorry I have to leave," Diana said. "There's so much I feel I haven't done or seen."

"All the more reason to return someday, Diana," Pascale said as they arrived at her home. She pulled the car around to the back of the house and backed it into a tiny space.

"You're sure it's okay that I'm already dressed and made up?" Diana asked, feeling self-conscious in the bright afternoon sun. For some reason, she felt her dress and makeup belonged more to a time after sundown.

"It's fine! Diana, everything will be great. You'll like my friends, and I'm very glad you agreed to stay overnight. Here," she said, opening the back door. "Take your time to settle in, then come find me in the front, say in about an hour. We can chat until the guests arrive." She started down the hallway, but paused and turned back, just as Diana was entering the apartment, Mulligan's old apartment. "You look really pretty, Diana."

❧

There were nine in total, including Pascale and her husband George. There was a couple from the university, Massimo and Rosa (he taught art history and she lectured on Swiss policy). Another couple came from a town called Neyruz (Paul was a marriage counselor and Sonja was a radiologist).

One of the unattached men, Teague, from Scotland originally, drank too much of the whiskey he'd brought for Pascale and George, and he barely made it through dinner. The other, Edouard, stayed sober throughout the evening and seemed genuinely interested in Diana.

"Where did you go to school?" she asked, preferring

to have him talk about himself so that she wouldn't have to tell him any of her own sordid life story.

"Strasbourg, are you familiar with it?" He was attractive, Diana thought, and he smelled fresh and citrusy, like summer. "But when I was younger, I spent some time at the Eccell Institute. In Montreux. I don't know if you would have ever heard of it." He cocked his head just a tiny bit, as if he were opening his ear to take in everything she would say.

"I've heard of the Eccell Institute, yes," she said, smiling. "In fact, I almost applied for a summer job there." *No need to elaborate.* "Strasbourg? It's near Germany, isn't it?"

"That's right!" He seemed so pleased that Diana knew where Strasbourg was located. Maybe he thought that Americans didn't know, or didn't care, about European geography. Diana was determined to impress him.

"What did you study there?"

"Biotechnology." He took a long drink from a glass of beer.

"Biotechnology? I've never heard of it," Diana said.

"In a simple form, we use microorganisms. There are needs in the fields of agriculture, food science, and medicine."

Diana stared at him. Edouard was cute, and he was really smart, smart in an area she couldn't even begin to discuss with him. Perhaps he sensed it, too.

"I work at Alcon, an eye care company. It's all quite boring, Diana, and I'd much rather talk about *you*." He gazed into her eyes until she had to look away. She felt a warm flush creep up her neck to her cheeks.

Pascale stood up and looked around the table. "I think we'll take a break and have dessert in the living room. Does everyone drink coffee?"

"Let me assist you," Diana said, rushing to help pick up plates.

"Nonsense," Pascale whispered. "George and I will do it. Go, go and spend time with Edouard." She winked at Diana. "I think he likes you!"

"I'm leaving in two weeks, Pascale. What good would it be to start something tonight?"

Pascale took Diana's elbow and dragged her into the kitchen, away from Edouard and the other guests. "Don't think about it! He's handsome, he's nice. Look, Teague is passed out, and he wasn't a good match for you, anyway. Diana," she pleaded, looking deep into Diana's eyes. "I want you to have good memories of this place and your time here. Go have a little fun." And with that, Pascale gently pushed Diana back out of the kitchen. Edouard stood at the dining room table, waiting for her. He was tall and straight. His clothes fit him nicely and he smelled great. He was mannered and thoughtful, and Diana fit a slight stirring inside, not a great rush of hormones but rather a deliberate glow that emanated from the pit of her stomach.

Diana watched Pascale and her husband, George, move about the kitchen, as if they were part of a highly choreographed dance. Pascale whispered to George and he nodded, then bumped her hip with his. Diana turned away. There was an intimacy between them that she envied. She'd never seen anything like it between her mother and father. Edouard waited by the table in the dining room. When she caught his eye, he lifted his eyebrows and the corners of his very nice mouth turned up. She wouldn't tell him any of her secrets: not her criminal father, her depressed mother, the fact that she had no money. She wouldn't talk about the Brusadins and their dysfunction, and she definitely wouldn't say anything about Luigi. She took three steps back to him.

"Edouard, you asked about me. Well, I'm from Newport," she said. "In Rhode Island. I'm flying back to the States at the end of this month." She bit her lower lip, then cringed at the thought of leaving lipstick on her teeth. She'd been so careful while she was eating. "I just thought you should know." She quickly ran her tongue over her teeth and hoped for the best. Will my imminent departure be a deal-breaker? He took her hand in his. Diana invoked a silent prayer that her hand was dry and cool, much like his, which was bigger, and felt so wonderful.

"It's a warm evening. Would you like to take a walk down the boulevard? I'm sure we will return in time for coffee and sweets."

"I'd love to. As long as I can change out of these high heels. I'll be right back." She pulled off her shoes and sprinted down the hallway to her room.

TWENTY-FIVE

Edouard telephoned Diana on Sunday evening, after she had returned to the Brusadins' house. Monsieur's eyebrows were raised all the way up his high forehead.

"Is it not a little late to start with a boyfriend, Diana?" He snickered at his joke, but Diana grabbed the telephone receiver out of his hand.

Diana put her index finger to her lips and scowled at him. He gave her a 'what, me?' look that she imagined Kenny would be using in no time. As he walked back to the living room to join Madame on the sofa, Diana turned her back to them and said in a low voice, "Hello?"

"Diana, it's Edouard. I hope I didn't disturb you."

"Not at all! I'm so glad you called. The man I work for was just being...silly."

"Ah, yes. Well, I simply wanted to tell you what an enjoyable time I had with you last night at Pascale's."

Diana felt, she actually felt her heart lift within her chest. *Why, oh why, do I have to leave the country in two weeks?* "I enjoyed it, too, Edouard. Very much."

"Would you like to have dinner on Friday this week? Can you get away?"

"Yes, I would, and yes, I can. Whatever work needs to be done is finished at the end of the day." Diana leaned against the wall. She could hear Madame and Monsieur talking in the next room. Kenny was asleep, and the television was turned down low. "You still want to, even though I have to go home at the end of this month?"

Edouard chuckled on the other end. "I'm glad you said yes," he replied, ignoring her statement. *A little fling? Is that what he wants? No,* she thought, *not with him. I won't have a casual relationship with him.*

"I will call for you on Friday at six then. I will be busy attending a conference in Ascona until Thursday; otherwise, I would call earlier. Pascale let me know where to find you, I hope that's all right."

Diana couldn't keep a grin from splitting her face. *Pascale, of course.* "I'm really looking forward to seeing you."

"As am I, Diana. Sleep well. Good night."

Diana replaced the telephone receiver in its cradle. She peeked around the corner at Madame. Her long legs were resting on Monsieur's thighs. Her eyes were closed and she was smiling. Diana didn't think she had ever seen Madame look so...content. Yes, she looked content.

"*Bonne nuit,*" she said softly, raising her hand.

Madame lifted a hand in reply, while Monsieur stared at Diana. She retreated to her bedroom, beaming like a child.

❧

Madame was in a good mood all week. Joyous, it might even seem. She laughed. She glowed. She touched Monsieur frequently, on the shoulder, the forearm, the cheek. She ran her fingers through his shaggy hair, she rested her palm on the top of his thigh while they sat together on the sofa in the evenings. And Diana changed their sheets every morning.

Finally, on Saturday at noon, while Diana was still smiling from her dinner date with Edouard, she was clued in, with Madame spilling out French like a nervous but happy schoolgirl and Monsieur smiling, translating what Diana couldn't understand. She learned that Madame had decided to start her own interior design business.

"Oh! That's wonderful. *Félicitations!*"

That was big news, Diana thought. *No wonder she's happy. She will get out from under Madame Portmann's dictatorial leadership. She will finally be free of her*, Diana thought happily.

"*Oui, on est très heureux.*" We are very happy.

"We *are* happy," Monsieur said, patting his wife's leg. "And I will be working with her," he added.

Whoa. Together? These two? Madame finally has a chance to express herself, to hone her identity, and she's going to have him next to her?

"No more insurance?" Diana asked Monsieur.

Monsieur waved away the question as if it, or Diana, was a pesky fly. "Luigi, do you remember Luigi?"

Monsieur's expression told her that he knew nothing of the assault. Diana kept her face placid even as her shaking legs threatened to give way beneath her. "He and his wife are in Italy, in Domodossola. For the baby." He used his hands to simulate a rounded belly. "So, I go into business with my wife! We are, what you call, partners!" He clapped Madame on the shoulder and Diana saw her wince.

Diana uncrossed her arms and willed herself to say nothing against their plan. *Not my business*, she kept repeating silently. She wished them both well and wondered how long the partnership would last. But she had to admit she'd never seen Madame look so happy.

TWENTY-SIX

It was Monday, one week before the last day of August, the day Diana would fly home. One more week to go. Edouard had taken Diana to Lausanne the previous day, on Sunday, and they had spent the day at the lake, walking along the promenade, dining on fresh-caught lake fish, and drinking good wine from the Valais region. Diana had still not told Edouard anything about her father, even when he had asked. She knew their little romance would end soon. What point was there in trying to continue a relationship with him in Switzerland and her in the States? And when would she ever be able to return to Switzerland? *Take it for what it is, Diana*, she told herself.

Still, they had talked about a lot of other things, even if Edouard's interests were so far above Diana's comprehension that she had a hard time keeping up. Allergies and immunology, infectious diseases, immunoregulation—what did it all mean? The most she could offer when Edouard asked about her interests was to tell him about her undergraduate degree in Art History.

"Do you think you might wish to go further with your studies?"

"Maybe. I mean, I was hoping to land a job in the Newport Museum, but it didn't pan out." She didn't say anything about tuition for graduate school.

"Perhaps you could get a job at one of the museums in Washington, DC, then think about enrolling in a program there. Maybe at Georgetown."

"In Washington?"

"Yes, in Washington." Edouard lifted one shoulder and gave Diana the tiniest of smiles. "Something to think about."

"Yes, I suppose," she replied. She felt Edouard reach for her hand.

"Please say you will think about it, Diana."

She looked into his eyes. *Why should he care, and why try to get her to apply for a job in DC?* Sure, there were better museums there, and her chances of landing one of only a couple of positions at the Newport Museum were tiny. If she ended up back with her mother in Providence, she could see if Brown University was hiring. But her mother had already said there was no room for her. Diana felt the pinprick of tears threatening, and blinked hard to keep them at bay. She fidgeted with the sleeve of her blouse.

"Diana. Something is troubling you. Can you talk to me?"

She lifted her chin and swallowed hard. She couldn't escape the truth. When she finally spoke, she couldn't look at him directly.

"Edouard, we don't know each other that well, and

I've deliberately not told you much about my family, because I have to fly home next week." She ventured a glance at his face and all she could see there was compassion. Bit by bit, she told him her story—about her growing up, her mother and father, her little brothers. And why she came to Switzerland in April, what her great plan had been, and how it had all gone very wrong.

"My father will spend time in prison. My mother wants nothing to do with him, and she has moved with my brothers to a small apartment far from where I grew up by the sea. I have no idea what is waiting for me when I get back. And my future is so uncertain...I'm sorry. You see why I didn't want to tell you?"

"I'm glad you did tell me, Diana."

"Really?" Edouard might have been glad, Diana thought, but she didn't feel any better.

❧

Mulligan wired five hundred dollars to Diana, and the very next day, Diana walked into the Kuoni travel agency and purchased a one-way ticket to Boston for the first day of September. The cheapest fare required her to take a train to Brussels, which meant an overnight stay in an unfamiliar city. But Pascale had a friend in Brussels and made a call on Diana's behalf.

"You go and stay with my friend Elisabeth, Diana. She will meet you at the station."

"That's too kind, Pascale. Thank you."

"It's nothing, my dear. You need a place to stay. And when you are older and very successful," she said with a wink, "you will remember this and you will help out a young person in need, yes?"

"Yes." Diana touched her index finger to the corner of her eye. "I don't know what's waiting for me at home, Pascale. Everything is...not what it was. I'm nervous. I can't explain it," she said.

Pascale opened her arms and Diana crawled into the embrace. "You don't have to explain, Diana. I know," she whispered.

Diana pulled back. "You do?"

"Some of it, yes, of course. Mulligan let me know about the situation with your family." Pascale stepped back and opened a cupboard in the kitchen. She withdrew a long white envelope and offered it to Diana. "Take this, please, Diana. George and I have been very successful in our lives. This...*misfortune*...it is your father's misfortune, not yours. You will remember that, yes?"

Diana nodded as Pascale pressed the envelope into her hand. "Yes. Thank you again, Pascale. For everything. You've been so kind to me."

"You finish out your obligation to *la famille Brusadin*. You have done well, Diana. I think you have grown up a lot in these short months. I can see that. And if you need a ride to the train station, you call me and I will come to get you."

Diana didn't open the envelope until much later that

evening, when she was alone in her little room. She held her breath and counted the bills. Pascale had given her enough money to rent an apartment of her own for at least six months.

❧

On the last Saturday in August, Diana awoke to a brilliant day. She had left the heavy metal shade up the previous evening, and sun poured into her east-facing bedroom window. She dressed, washed her face, and headed to the kitchen. Her last Saturday in the little white house. She would work until noon, but had no plans for the rest of the day. Madame had said they would all go to a restaurant in the neighboring town of Tafers to celebrate the Brusadins' new venture and to thank Diana for her service.

Diana was in the kitchen, cleaning the counters and appliances, when she heard a car door slam. *What did Monsieur say about Luigi and his wife going to Domodossola? They're gone, aren't they?* She ran into her bedroom, where she could look out her open window to the driveway below. A man in a dark business suit, unusual for a Saturday, got out of the car, and Monsieur walked out to greet him in the driveway. Standing to the side of the open window, Diana watched their body language— the man stood perfectly still, a folder in his left hand, and Monsieur looked agitated as he raised his arms. She couldn't hear what they were saying, but Monsieur's voice was raised while the other man stayed calm. *"Non! Ce n'est pas vrai!"* Diana knew Madame was in the back yard with Kenny. What was going on? Was Monsieur in trouble? Diana felt a hole in the pit of her stomach, spreading, like a virus.

The man in the suit held out some papers, then shook them at Monsieur. Monsieur grabbed the papers and the man got into his car. He backed up as the chickens scurried away. Diana watched Monsieur watch the departing car. He looked down at the papers again before he turned to walk around the house to the back yard. With his thinning hair and slumped shoulders, he looked much older than forty. As Diana tiptoed from her bedroom, she could hear Madame through the screen door, asking questions, her voice rising. She still couldn't tell what they were saying, and Madame was talking fast, in an unusually high-pitched voice. *I should check on Kenny.* If Madame and Monsieur were about to have a fight, she'd bring Kenny inside, away from it. She knew she couldn't shield him from their arguments once she was gone, but she wasn't gone yet. *Madame had been so happy! What the heck was going on?*

As Diana walked through the house to the back yard, she saw Kenny, sitting alone on the grass, clutching his stuffed rabbit, working his pacifier furiously. He stared up at Diana as she approached. Madame and Monsieur had gone down to the driveway, away from Kenny, but Diana couldn't hear anything. No yelling, that was good. She looked down at Kenny and he raised his arms to her. She scooped him up and brought him inside, where she held him in her lap, waiting. *Something bad has happened*, she thought. Her first instinct was to blame Monsieur, but that wasn't fair, she knew. He had yelled back at the man, that whatever the man had said wasn't true. Perhaps there was an accusation against him? Something to do with the insurance he sold?

Then, she heard a car door slam again and Monsieur yelled something unintelligible before squealing out of the driveway. Diana tensed her entire body, all while stroking Kenny's back. She watched as Madame came into view in the back yard, looking frantic as she searched for her son.

"*Madame! Ici!*" Diana called. Madame pulled aside the screen sliding door and looked relieved to see Kenny.

"*Donne-le moi, Diana*," she cried. Give him to me.

Obligingly, Diana handed him over, and Madame dropped into the rocking chair, holding Kenny tightly against her chest. He had yet to utter a sound, but his dark eyes were enormous.

"What is it? *Qu'est-ce que c'est?*"

Madame's eyes were glistening, but her mouth was set in a hard line. In French, she spoke, and her voice was edged with bitter weariness. "My husband has a child, a daughter, from a previous...relationship. The girl is fourteen." Madame rocked Kenny, whose big brown eyes had grown heavy-lidded with the steady motion of the chair. "He is obligated to pay support for her, every month. But he has not paid. For *three years* he has not paid." She held up her thumb and two fingers. "He always assured me that he had paid."

Diana drew in a sharp breath. Three years of child support! That would be a lot of money, she assumed. So Monsieur had been lying to her, for years.

"I'm so sorry," Diana murmured. *"Je suis vraiment désolée."*

Madame continued to rock back and forth. She stared out the glass sliding door at the back of the house, to the expanse of land on the other side of the fence. A black and white cow stood, chewing grass, swatting away flies with sharp flicks of its tail.

"Je déteste vivre ici," she said. Diana was grateful she could understand Madame. She said she hated living here. *"Les mouches."* Yes, Diana thought. The flies were everywhere. She knew Madame hated them. Diana hated them, too.

"Partout," Diana said, indicating to Madame that not only did she understand, she agreed with her.

"Tu sais ce que les mouches mangent? De la merde. Elles mangent de la merde, Diana, *et on vit juste à côté. Je déteste vivre ici,"* she muttered, letting her tears run down her cheeks.

Madame was right. The flies were everywhere, and they feasted on cow shit, and the house was right in the middle of it all. No wonder she hated it.

"I'm sorry," Diana said again. She had no idea what all of it meant, but she guessed that Madame's dream of starting her own design business was no longer possible.

How could she, if they needed to pay back so much money? *What had Monsieur done?*

"*Attention aux hommes,*" Madame spat. Be careful of men. She went on to say that princes didn't exist. Even the wedding they had just watched on television last month? "*Charles et Diana?*" She blew out a bitter puff of air. "*N'y croyez pas. Les contes de fées n'existent pas.*" Don't believe it. Fairy tales don't exist.

Diana knew that if she had learned anything from the past four and a half months, it was that. There were no princes. There were no fairy tales. But she still hoped that Charles and Diana would prove her wrong.

TWENTY-SEVEN

Monsieur did not return home that evening, and Madame and Diana ate fruit and drank wine for dinner. Madame drank most of the wine. Obviously, the restaurant trip was out, and Diana called Pascale on Saturday evening, after she'd helped put Madame to bed. Diana had allowed Kenny to sleep in the bed with Madame, and had decided to stay up all night, with Madame's bedroom door open, just in case she was needed. When Pascale picked up the phone, Diana immediately apologized for the late call. Then she told Pascale everything that had happened.

"Oh no. Do you want me to come get you now?"

"No," Diana whispered into the phone. She looked around the house, searing images into her mind. "I haven't packed yet, and I don't even know if Monsieur will come home tonight. If he doesn't, I need to stay here. But tomorrow morning if you can. Madame will have to understand. I need to get out of the house."

"Yes, I think you do. I'll be by around nine-thirty, is that all right with you?"

"Thank you, Pascale, I'll see you then. Oh, Pascale? Would you do me one last favor?"

❧

It rained all night, and Diana couldn't sleep even if she had wanted to. She heard Monsieur come home around three in the morning—first the key in the lock at the front door, then the door opening, then the door closing. She heard him urinate in the WC, the room with the poster of Julio Iglesias on the door. She heard him flush, then the faucet. She lay still and listened as he walked to his bedroom door, which Diana had left ajar. She heard him close the door.

Diana tensed, and waited for shouts, yelling, Kenny waking and crying, but she heard nothing. Still, she lay awake most of the night.

❧

On Sunday morning, Diana folded her clothes carefully, making everything fit in her suitcases. She stripped her bed and mounded the sheets and pillowcase at the foot of the bed. She listened at the door before opening it wide. There were no sounds inside, only birdsong from the robins and thrushes in the trees around the house.

She brought her suitcases to the foyer and set them down beside the front door. It was seven o'clock, and everyone should have been up, even though it was Sunday. Madame was probably still sleeping off the effects of her drinking, and Monsieur? He had come home at three in the morning. Diana walked softly to Kenny's room. He was in his crib, awake but quiet, perhaps innately aware of the tumult between his parents. She hadn't heard any noises the previous night, but someone, probably Monsieur, had brought him into his room and put him in his crib. *Children are perceptive*, she thought. *This poor kid. What does his future look like?* She lifted him to the changing table.

"You need to start using the toilet, Kenny, like a big boy."

He stared at her. "Eye-ah."

"That's right. I am 'Eye-ah.' You are Kenny. Kennee." That improbable name. Because his father liked Kenny Rogers and "The Gambler." Of course he did. He probably couldn't even sing all the lyrics. Besides, it was Madame who really needed to know when to hold 'em and when to walk away. It was the secret to surviving, as Kenny Rogers would sing.

Diana hoisted Kenny to her hip and carried him into the kitchen, where she poured some juice and took a croissant from the covered box. As they sat together in the dining room, Diana checked her watch. She almost wished Pascale would come earlier and take her away.

It was August thirtieth, and Diana was leaving, one day before her technical last day, but she didn't care. What were they going to do, fire her? She had told Madame that she would stay with Pascale and George on Sunday, and take a train to Brussels on Monday, but Diana wagered Madame wouldn't remember. Sunday was her day off.

She could have, probably should have, gone to Pascale's the previous evening, but she couldn't leave Madame. Or Kenny. After what had transpired with Monsieur, Diana didn't have the nerve. Then Madame had drunk herself into a stupor. And Kenny. Poor little Kenny. *I'll wake Madame and Monsieur if I have to.* She wasn't going to just pick up her suitcases and leave.

The previous night, as Kenny had dozed on the rug, Diana sat with Madame. They were still on their first glass of wine. Madame asked her what she was going to do once she returned home.

"*Je ne suis pas encore sûre,*" Diana said, after telling Madame she was leaving the next day. I'm not yet sure. Edouard had planted a seed about applying for a job in Washington, and Diana had been thinking about it. A chance to move away, start a new life. More opportunities in Washington, DC, plenty of museums. "*Je ne sais pas.*"

Madame had nodded, her head like one of those springy dolls Diana had seen on someone's dashboard once. "*Oui,*" she'd replied. She gazed at Diana through red-rimmed eyes. Her mascara was all cried off and Madame looked vulnerable, younger even, without the severe black eyeliner. "*Et le jeune homme?*"

Diana's face gave her away, the silly grin she'd had all week. But she answered, "*Il reste ici. Je pars.*" He is staying here. I'm leaving.

Madame shrugged, as if nothing would ever work out well in her world. She told Diana that she had wanted to give her some money, but the words trailed off. "*Mais maintenant...*" But now...

There was no money. Diana knew that song by heart.

⁂

Diana checked her watch. Pascale would arrive to pick her up in less than an hour.

"*Bonjour,*" Madame murmured. She padded into the kitchen on bare feet. "*Ça va?*" She smiled down at Kenny and ruffled his curls.

"*Oui, ça va,* Madame." Diana stayed seated. It was her last morning, and it was Sunday. She didn't work for them anymore.

"*J'ai la gueule de bois,*" Madame said sheepishly. She giggled and raked a hand through unkempt hair.

"*Une gueule de bois?*" A mouth of wood?

Madame laid a palm against her temple. "*Trop de vin.*" Too much wine.

"Ah! Yes, a mouth of wood." A new expression for a hangover. Great, Diana thought, a phrase I hope I never have to use. "We say '*une bouche en coton.*'"

Madame prepared coffee in the kitchen, then returned her focus to Kenny. Lifting her still-swollen eyes to Diana, she said in French, "I'm sorry about yesterday."

"*Pourquoi?*" Why? *She hadn't done anything wrong,* Diana thought. Her over-drinking was because of the significance of the situation with Monsieur.

"*Je l'ai épousé.*" I married him. She continued in French. "I'm not going to leave him, Diana. Kenny needs his father. Giancarlo is a good father."

"Okay," Diana replied. "*Votre décision.*" Emboldened, she asked, "*Et votre nouvelle entreprise?*" What about your new design company?

Madame's face stiffened as she set her jaw. "*Non. Pas possible maintenant.*" Of course not, Diana thought. They had all that money to pay, because of Monsieur's wrongdoing. Thanks to him, she'll have to forego her dream. Madame lowered her eyes and ran her fingers through Kenny's curls. "*Peut-être un jour.*"

Yes, maybe someday.

TWENTY-EIGHT

Pascale arrived shortly before nine-thirty, and Diana was relieved. She held Kenny in her arms while he squirmed against her. "Be a good boy for *Maman*," she whispered into his hair. "*Je t'aime.*"

Kenny stilled and put his tiny hand against Diana's cheek. "Eye-ah."

Blinking hard, Diana gave the boy back to Madame. "*Au revoir, Madame Brusadin,*" she said, kissing her three times, the Swiss way. Monsieur had not emerged from his bedroom, and Diana was just as glad not to see him. She was sure he was awake—there was too much noise when Pascale arrived. *No*, Diana thought, *he's a coward*.

Madame, in a gesture reminiscent of Kenny, touched Diana's cheek and said, "*Au revoir, Diana. Bonne chance.*"

"Good luck to you, too." Diana looked meaningfully into Madame's eyes. "Thank you. *Merci. Pour les leçons de vie.*" For the life lessons.

"Okay, time to go?" Pascale said. She picked up the larger of Diana's suitcases with her left hand and shook Madame's outstretched hand with her right. As Pascale led the way down the stone steps to the driveway, Diana heard the front door close behind her.

Before she climbed into Pascale's car, Diana glanced up at Monsieur's bedroom window, but the shades were down. Nothing.

※

That evening, Pascale and George brought Diana to a restaurant in town. "I'm sorry Edouard couldn't join us," Pascale said. "He was very sorry that he was delayed in Bern, but he had an important meeting."

Diana looked at Pascale with skepticism. A meeting on a Sunday evening? Really, Edouard, you couldn't come up with something better than that?

Seeing the look on Diana's face, Pascale pressed her. "What is it?"

Diana traced a circle on the white linen tablecloth. She glanced up at George, a man she didn't know well but who smiled benevolently at her. Pascale had genuine concern on her face. "It's hard. We've gotten on so well these past weeks, and now I go back home. I knew it would be difficult, but I had hoped we could see each other one last time. He and I had talked about one final chance to get together, but I guess his meeting, if that's really what it is, was more important." She stopped herself. "Forget it, I'm being a spoiled brat. I knew this would end, and I tried not to like him too much!" She forced a smile. "But I really do like him."

"Diana, you never know what the future will bring to you. Be open to accept new chances and opportunities."

She didn't know what Pascale meant, but accepted her words willingly.

※

The next morning, the last day of August, Pascale walked with Diana to the train station. Pascale paused outside the entrance.

"Thank you for coming with me," Diana said. "Can you stay? My train doesn't arrive for over thirty minutes. Please, let me buy you a coffee. It's the least I can do."

Pascale placed one hand over her heart. "There's someone inside waiting for you," she said. "I'll say goodbye now." She opened her arms for a last embrace and squeezed Diana tightly.

"Who's waiting—oh! Truly, Pascale?"

"Truly. Go find him. And safe travels, Diana."

Diana watched Pascale turn and stride down the street, back to her house. She bent to pick up her suitcases.

"Let me help," Edouard said.

"Edouard! What are you doing here?" she exclaimed. When they had said goodbye the previous weekend, Diana assumed their brief romance was over. And when he didn't show up at the restaurant the previous evening, Diana made an assumption that Edouard was ready to be done with her.

"I'm sorry I couldn't join you with Pascale and George last night. I had a meeting, one that was very important."

So that was the truth? Diana, stop doubting people.

"So Pascale said. I can't believe you're here!"

"Come on, let's have a quick coffee. I have something to tell you."

Once they were seated and served, Edouard leaned forward in his chair.

"Diana, you remember I asked you to think about applying for a job at one of the museums in Washington, DC?"

"Yes, of course. I've thought of nothing else since then."

"And you like the idea?"

"Yes. I think you're right, the opportunities are better there. As soon as I get home, I'll start on that."

"You have the proper qualifications, and I may have a contact who can help you, too." At Diana's questioning look, Edouard continued. "My sister-in-law is an administrator at the National Gallery of Art. I have already made an inquiry on your behalf, and she would very much like to speak with you."

"What? You did that for me?" Diana stared at him. A tingling began in her toes and slowly made its way upwards.

He shrugged. "I thought that if you were not interested, it would still be okay. But I hoped you would be interested." He made a sign of crossing his fingers.

"But why? Why such an interest in Washington?"

Edouard adjusted his eyeglasses. "Well, that is my news, Diana. Why I had a meeting last evening. I have been offered a job. In Washington, DC. There is a place called the National Institute of Allergy and Infectious Diseases, and there is a new chief of the Laboratory of Immunoregulation. He is actually a distant cousin of mine, through our grandparents." Edouard brightened. "I think we would say he is a first cousin once removed." He looked pleased to be able to put it that way.

"Really? You're going to work there?"

"I am, Diana. I'm very excited about it, and although I wasn't sure if I would get the job, I wanted to give you something to think about, in case I did."

Diana was reeling. She looked down at her hands. They were trembling.

Edouard must have seen it, too, because he reached for them, taking both of her hands in his own. "Diana. I wanted you to leave Switzerland with a happy heart. With a hopeful heart."

She knew she would. She would leave with a happy, hopeful heart. An irrepressible and impassioned hopefulness, a radiant happiness.

Edouard checked his watch. "Come on, Diana. It's time." He tossed some coins on the table to pay for the coffee, and lifted Diana's suitcases. Together they walked up the stairs to her platform.

"I wish you a good flight, Diana," Edouard said softly. He pulled a folded piece of paper from his pocket and tucked it into her hand. "There are many telephone numbers on this paper. Three for me, one for my sister-in-law. We will speak very soon, I know."

Diana looked up at his face and struggled to find the words she wanted to say.

He smiled down at her. "Do you know the expression '*la vie en rose*'? It is to see life in pink, as it were. To see the brighter side of life, Diana. This is what I want for you, to be optimistic about the future. About our future. Yes?"

"Yes. Yes indeed, Edouard."

ACKNOWLEDGMENTS

In 2019, I had finished my ninth book, *All's Well in Jingle Valley*, and had some ideas about a new novel. As my readers know, I love Switzerland and have set four of my nine books there. Around Christmastime in 2019, I told my husband I had one more book in me that would be set in Switzerland, based upon a summer I spent, after college, working as an *au pair* for a small family in a small town in Switzerland.

This book would be different from the Swiss Chocolate trilogy I had published, and different also from *Villa del Sol*, which is set primarily in Lugano, Switzerland, near the Italian border. I asked my husband if he thought it was a good idea to write one more book about Switzerland, and not only was he enthusiastic, but he also offered to send me to Switzerland so I could do a little research.

I made plans for a brief trip, and coordinated with a couple of my Swiss friends to catch up while I was there. I booked a flight for March 8, 2020 and planned to stay in my beloved town of Fribourg for eight days.

Well, we all know what happened in March. As pandemic concerns and cases grew, we talked a lot about whether I should go. But we both felt that as long as I was keeping mostly to myself, I'd be okay. Switzerland was in good shape—its first case, at the end of February, was in the Lugano region, and I had no plans to travel anywhere near Lugano. But just three days after my arrival in Fribourg, due to announcements by the former president and legitimate concerns from my husband, I was packing my bags to return home. Because while I do love Switzerland, I love my husband more. I waited in crowded airports at Zurich and Dublin, sat in airplanes full of unmasked passengers, and arrived back home in Boston many hours later, sleepless and nervous. Very fortunately, I did not get sick, nor did my husband, nor did anyone in my immediate family. We are all so grateful for that.

During my very brief stay in Switzerland, I was able to meet up with my good friend Barbara Green-Studer, who offered to help me find the house at the edge of the farm where I had worked. It was raining, and I stood in the gravel driveway, staring up at the house. I was overcome with memories of happy and not-happy-at-all times. Later that day, Barbara and her husband Jean-Bernard welcomed me into their home, and even though we were aware of COVID-19, we believed we were being careful. (Thankfully, neither Barbara nor Jean-Bernard got sick).

I did miss seeing my new friend Halley Gentil and my good friend of many years Fabiola Dreyer-Abbet, but Halley and I still keep in touch, and Fabiola has been instrumental in proofing my foreign words and phrases, as she did for *Villa del Sol*. I am so grateful.

Thank you to Ryan Lanz of The Book Review Directory. I've been working with Ryan for years now, and am grateful for his assistance in crafting the back cover copy for this novel.

I am a proud member of the Association of Rhode Island Authors, a 300+-member group of Rhode Island authors and poets. There is so much talent within the perimeter of our little state! Through this organization, I've met some of the best people I'd ever want to be professionally associated with. Even as an author with this, my tenth book, there's always more to learn about writing and marketing, and ARIA provides all of that.

I'm also affiliated with the Independent Publishers of New England (IPNE), an organization of professionals, authors, and companies who collaborate to help each other learn and succeed in the independent book publishing field.

Thank you to Stillwater River Publications and its owners (and my friends), Steve and Dawn Porter. You won't find two better people to work with, and I am so thrilled to be a writer whose work is published by Stillwater.

My online writing and reading community continues to grow, and I'm happy and proud to be affiliated with Readers Coffeehouse, Bookish Road Trip, Every Damn Day Writers, and Bookworms Anonymous Authors Group.

Thank you for reading my books! It's *you*, treasured reader, who keeps me going. It's because you read and enjoy my books that I keep writing. And I am so very thankful to be able to do this thing I love.

Made in United States
North Haven, CT
27 July 2023

39580760R00117